STAY WITH ME
Forever

Farrah Rochon

HARLEQUIN® KIMANI™ ROMANCE

ISBN-13: 978-0-373-86414-0

Stay with Me Forever

HARLEQUIN®

Printed in U.S.A.

™ www.Harlequin.com

Farrah Rochon had dreams of becoming a fashion designer as a teenager, until she discovered she would be expected to wear something other than jeans to work every day. Thankfully, the coffee shop where she writes does not have a dress code. When Farrah is not penning stories, the *USA TODAY* bestselling author and avid sports fan feeds her addiction to football by attending New Orleans Saints games.

Books by Farrah Rochon

Harlequin Kimani Romance

Huddle with Me Tonight

I'll Catch You

Field of Pleasure

Pleasure Rush

A Forever Kind of Love

Always and Forever

Delectable Desire

Runaway Attraction

Yours Forever

Forever's Promise

A Mistletoe Affair

Forever with You

Stay with Me Forever

Visit the Author Profile page at Harlequin.com for more titles.

Dedicated to Dr. Y. Dubois Williams, who once told me
that if I wanted to be a writer, I should be a writer.
So I did.

Commit your work to the Lord,
and your plans will be established.
—*Proverbs* 16:3

Chapter 1

The newspaper Paxton Jones held over her head was no match for the fat raindrops being pelted from the storm clouds hovering in the gray skies. She tossed the useless shield onto the backseat, cursing her bad habit of forgetting to put her umbrella back in the car after she used it.

"Girl, get out of that rain before you catch a cold!"

Paxton looked over her shoulder to find her mother standing on the narrow porch that surrounded what, up until this weekend, was known to the people of Gauthier, Louisiana, as Harlon's Bar. Over the past three days, the fifty-five-year-old clapboard structure had undergone a massive overhaul, complete with a new owner and a brand-new name: the River Road Bar and Grille.

At least that was the official name on the new deed, but Paxton had never been one to kid herself. She knew it would take an act of Congress to convince the longtime residents in Landreaux—which was technically still part of Gauthier but was divided from the rest of the town by Landreaux Creek—to call this place anything but Harlon's. If they were lucky, maybe she and her mother could eventually cajole them into calling it Belinda's, but Paxton wasn't holding her breath.

"You're going to get sick," her mother called again. "Get in here!"

"Give me just a minute," Paxton called back to her.

Scooping up the bags of cleaning supplies she'd just purchased from the Gauthier Pharmacy and Feed Store, she dashed from her Lincoln MKX to the bar's newly installed wooden steps. As she made her way up to the small landing, Paxton slipped on the second to last step, nearly dumping the bags.

"Watch it," Belinda Jones said, reaching out for her.

"I've got it." Paxton righted herself. "But maybe you should add installing nonskid protectors to the list of things that need to be done before the bar's grand re-opening."

"You're probably right," Belinda said. She gestured for Paxton to go ahead of her as they walked through the gaping hole where the new door would be hung as soon as Rickey Price finished constructing it at his cabinetry shop. "I'll call Nathan Robottom at the hardware store. I'm sure he'll have something we can use."

"Good," Paxton said. "Because after the blood, sweat and tears that you've put into this place, I won't allow a slip-and-fall lawsuit to ruin it all."

"We'll take care of the steps. I'm more concerned about you catching your death out here in this rain."

Just as Paxton opened her mouth to remind her mother

for the seven thousandth time that being caught in the rain did not automatically give you a cold, she coughed.

Perfect timing.

The I-told-you-so lift to Belinda's brow was a well-practiced, well-executed blast from Paxton's childhood. Make that her adulthood, too. Because at thirty-seven years old, she found it as effective as it had been when she was seven. It made her want to cringe.

"No need to break out the warm socks and hot tea," Paxton said. "I was clearing my throat. I don't have a cold."

"Not yet," her mother said with a lift to her chin.

Paxton released an overly exasperated sigh as she laughed at her mother's haughty expression.

"I'll take some cough syrup before I go to sleep tonight," she said. "Will that do, or do you have to take my temperature before you're satisfied?"

"So do they teach classes on how to sass your mama up there in Little Rock, or did you learn how to do that on your own?"

She barked out another sharp laugh. "If anyone taught me how to sass, it's the woman standing right in front of me."

Belinda winked. "You got that right." She reached for the plastic bags, but Paxton twisted them out of her reach.

"I've got this," she said as she started emptying the supplies she'd picked up during her quick trip to downtown Gauthier—items that would have cost about half of what she'd paid if she'd driven over to the new Target in neighboring Maplesville. Paxton prided herself on being a strong, independent woman who made her own decisions, but even she wasn't brave enough to walk into this bar carrying a red-and-white Target shopping bag. Her mother was firmly on the boycott-big-business bandwagon.

Paxton had not been in town for more than an hour before she had been presented with a pledge sheet that was being circulated by the Gauthier Civic Association to boycott the big-box store, along with several other establishments. Tensions between Gauthier and Maplesville had been simmering back when Paxton relocated to Arkansas a year ago, and the opening of yet another large national chain store that could take business away from Gauthier's mom-and-pop shops had only elevated the friction.

Paxton had been happy to sign the pledge. She felt it her duty to support the local businesses in her small hometown. Even more so now that her mother owned one.

Just thinking those words caused an excited tingle to rush through her. It was like a human-interest story worthy of one of those cheesy but sweet headlines.

Belinda Jones: From Bartender to Bar Owner.

Followed by Paxton Jones: Daughter of the Year.

Pretentious? Possibly, but she knew her mother would agree with her, and not just because Paxton had taken a sledgehammer to her 401(k) in order to purchase this bar. Belinda had placed the Daughter of the Year crown on Pax's head ever since she'd won third place in the fourth-grade spelling bee.

"You can check the final building inspection off your list," her mother, who had resumed her sweeping, said. "Josh Howard came over while you were out. He gave the place a clean bill."

"Without a front door?"

Belinda waved that off. "I told him it would be installed later today. Rickey is his second cousin on his mama's side—he knows he's good for it."

Paxton shook her head. "Gotta love a small town," she said as she stacked the sponges, all-purpose disinfecting spray and grout cleaner on one of the new pub tables that had been delivered that morning.

A loud whistle drew her attention to the left side of the bar.

"I knew I smelled trouble in the air."

Paxton grinned as Harlon Lewis, the bar's previous owner, entered through the side door entrance. He shucked off his raincoat, leaving it just inside the door. He was accompanied by his grandson, Donovan, who carried two large fleur-de-lis wall decor pieces crafted out of dented sheet metal and spray painted a shimmering metallic gold.

Paxton balled up the plastic shopping bags and tossed them in the blue recycle bin as she made her way over to Harlon. She wrapped her arms around his neck and gave him a loud kiss.

"It's so good to see you," she said. She leaned back and smiled up at the man who had been the only father figure she'd ever known. "I've missed you, old man. You weren't at the house when I dropped by yesterday."

"You gotta get there early to catch me, girlie. I've got places to be."

"Thanks for picking these up for me," she said, gesturing to the fleur-de-lis. She'd commissioned Gauthier's own metalworks artist and restoration specialist, Phylicia Phillips, to start making them as soon as the sale of the bar went through.

"It was no problem," Harlon said. "Phil's new shop ain't too far from the house."

"Still, you saved me a trip," Paxton said, plopping another peck on his cheek.

"Hey, where's my kiss?" His grandson Donovan asked, leaning toward her.

"Boy, get out of here with that mess." Harlon swatted him with the dusty Vietnam War vet baseball cap he'd been wearing for the better part of the three decades Paxton had known him.

Donovan frowned at his grandfather, then winked at Paxton.

"You can put those over there," Paxton pointed toward the bar, which had been freshly waxed earlier that day. "I have an *X* marked with electrical tape on the wall. You'll find a nail right above it that you can hang them on."

"Fine, but it'll cost you a kiss," Donovan said with another wink.

Paxton rolled her eyes and released a heavy sigh. This one would be a problem.

When she'd driven over to Harlon's house on the lake yesterday, she'd been informed by the twenty-two-year-old—whom she used to babysit for extra money back when she was in high school—that his grandfather was on a hunting trip. Donovan invited her to join him inside for a beer, an invitation Paxton had instantly turned down. It only made him more eager.

The little scrub had the nerve to tell her that he was going to make her his cougar. Paxton was so stunned by his boldness that she'd laughed in his face. She'd hoped her remarks about eating little tiger cubs like him for breakfast would have put an end to his pursuit, but apparently not.

While his grandson hung the artwork, Paxton threaded her arm through Harlon's and took him on a tour. A ribbon of pride curled around her as he remarked on all the changes that had been done in the past couple of days.

"Girl, you are amazing. You turned this old dump into a palace."

"This bar has never been a dump. You always took good care of it. We just spruced it up a bit."

"Spruced it up, my foot. This place looks a hundred times better than it did before. A thousand. You did good by your mama, girl. I'm proud of you. She deserves this."

Paxton barely managed to swallow the lump of emotion wedged in her throat. She coughed, ready to lay claim to the cold her mother had accused her of catching. Sentimental public displays had never been her style, and the sincerity in Harlon's voice brought her close to the brink.

"Owning her own place has been a dream of hers for a long time," Paxton said. "Thank you for selling it to us at such a reasonable price."

He waved that off. "I'm sorry I had to sell it to you at all. If I'd been better at tucking money away, I would have given it to her."

"She never would have taken it from you," Paxton said.

She and Belinda had a lot of things in common, but that stubborn streak of pride was, by far, the strongest thread tying them together. The Joneses did not accept charity. Ever. They worked hard for what they wanted, and if they couldn't get it on their own, then they weren't meant to have it.

Paxton had lived by that simple philosophy all her

life. It compelled her to never settle for second-best, because there was nothing like basking in the satisfaction of seeing your hard work pay off.

Like right now. The pure joy emanating from her mother as she swept a floor she'd swept thousands of times over the past two decades warmed every part of Paxton's heart, and it made all the hard work and sacrifice it would take to pay for this bar worth it.

"Look at that smile on her face," Paxton whispered in Harlon's ear as they both stared at her mother.

"Not sure when I last saw her like this. Maybe when you walked across the stage to pick up that fancy college degree." He nudged Paxton's shoulder. "You just make sure she lets me come in and work every now and then."

"She wouldn't let you work when you owned the place," Paxton said with a laugh. "I don't know why you think things would change now."

She guided Harlon to the new kitchen that had been added onto the bar. It had been under construction for the past month. With the installation of the three-part sink this morning, it was officially operational.

Donovan walked in and braced both hands high against the doorjamb. His shirt hem lifted slightly, exposing a set of tawny, well-defined abs. For a half second Paxton was intrigued, but then she remembered she used to change this kid's diapers.

The momentary flourish of awareness was an understandable physical reaction considering the drought she'd been in over the past six months. The handheld device she brought to bed at night wasn't doing the job it used to do.

"You need some help in here?" Donovan asked, winking again.

Then again, maybe she just needed to refresh the batteries.

"You'd better get that eye checked out," Paxton told him. "All that twitching can't be healthy."

He entered the kitchen, stepping up to her. "Why are you giving me such a hard time? I'm not a little boy anymore. I can rock your world."

Harlon knocked him upside the head with his baseball cap again.

"Dude." Donovan rubbed his ear. He scowled at his grandfather. "Stop blocking my game, Grandpa. I'm trying to get something going here."

"It will never happen," Paxton told him.

"We'll see," Donovan said, a cocky smile tilting up the corner of his mouth.

Harlon shook his head. "Hormones got that one acting a damn fool. If he gets too vexing once he starts working here, just strangle him."

"Hopefully he'll be too busy helping customers to bother me with his tired pickup lines," she said.

Her mother had hired Donovan to help out at the bar while he took yet another semester off from college to "explore his options." Paxton was about 96 percent sure that she would, in fact, have to strangle the little Casanova before she returned to Little Rock.

If she returned to Little Rock.

She stifled a sigh. She had only been back in town for two days and already the *should I stay, should I go back* dance was getting the best of her. It happened every single time she came home to visit. But Paxton knew it was better to have some distance between herself and Gauthier, especially now that a certain someone was back in town. Permanently.

The rumble of a diesel engine and tires crunching over gravel came through the open doorway, tearing her attention away from those thoughts she had no desire to explore at the moment.

"Finally," Paxton said, making her way past Donovan and through the kitchen. "That must be the TVs."

She exited the side door and rounded the front of the building, waving at the delivery truck driver. Thankfully, the rain had lightened to a steady but weaker sprinkle.

"Over here," Paxton called, waving her hands.

A loud bark came from just behind her a second before Heinz, the huge mutt she'd nursed back to health after he'd gotten into a fight with a coyote, came barreling into her legs. Paxton's fingers automatically scratched the scruff behind his ear.

"What in the world," Belinda said as she came down the stairs, followed closely by Harlon and Donovan. The four of them stood to the side, surveying the deliverymen as they carted a fifty-five-inch LCD TV into the building.

Harlon pointed to the delivery truck's raised gate. "What did you do, girl? Buy out the entire store?"

"You can't have a sports bar with that little black-and-white television behind the bar," Paxton said.

"How many TVs did you buy?" Belinda asked, her voice a combination of awe and trepidation.

Bracing herself for her mother's reaction, Paxton said, "Eight."

"Eight!" Belinda's screech echoed around the open clearing. "No, no, no." She held her hands out in an attempt to stop the deliverymen. They bypassed her and carried in the second television. "There's not enough room in this bar for eight TVs."

"We'll make them fit," Paxton said. "Oh, I forgot to mention that the guy from the satellite company will be a little late, but it should be installed by tonight."

"Oh, yeah," Donovan said, rubbing his hands together. "You got the football package?"

"Of course." Paxton nodded. "And I've already ordered the NBA package, too."

"This place is gonna be fiyah. Maybe I don't need to worry about college. I can just work here."

Belinda grasped Paxton's forearm and gave it a slight squeeze. "How much is all of this costing you?" she asked.

Despite the genuine concern in her mother's voice, Paxton ignored the question, just as she had ignored it the 542 times Belinda had inquired about the cost of all of this in the months since Harlon decided to retire and sell the bar.

She knew her mother was concerned about the money. She was *always* concerned about money. She'd tended bar at Harlon's for the past thirty-two years, and although Harlon had always paid her a fair wage, this little watering hole on the low-income side of Gauthier had never made enough to make anyone rich.

Barely scraping by had been a way of life for her mother for far too long. She'd sacrificed everything—food in her belly, clothes on her back, countless hours of sleep—all to make sure Paxton had an easier road than the one she'd traveled.

One could argue that Paxton had sacrificed just as much as her mother had. After all, she'd spent the better part of her adolescence working side by side with Belinda in this very bar. They were a team, always had been. But the few hours she spent helping out in the evenings and weekend here at Harlon's was nothing compared with the time and hard work Belinda had put in day after day, year after year.

That she could now afford to properly thank her mother for all she'd given up for her filled Paxton's chest with pride.

Which was why she refused to engage in any discussion of what all of this was costing her. As a project manager for one of the largest engineering firms in the Gulf South, she'd managed to build a nice nest egg in a relatively short amount of time. Sure, she'd emptied it in order to buy this place and renovate it, but Paxton had a set of career goals in front of her; she was confident she would be able to replenish her savings in a matter of a few short years. Especially if things went as she'd planned them out in her head.

"With all the money you've put into this place, you'll have to sell a lot of beer and tater skins to break even," Harlon remarked as the final television was carted through the door.

"Could we please close this subject?" Paxton said. "We still have a lot to do before the grand opening, and I've got to be at the Gauthier Law Firm early in the morning."

"What you got going on over there?" Harlon asked. "You need Matt Gauthier to get you out of a bind?"

Paxton shook her head. "Matt has been kind enough to let us use the extra conference room as a temporary office for the flood protection project I'm working on. I'm lucky that he had some available space."

At least Paxton thought she was lucky, until this past Thursday when she'd discovered that the state engineer who'd been assigned to the project had abruptly left the

Army Corps of Engineer Civil Works department. He'd been replaced by another civil engineer. Sawyer Robertson.

The muscles in her belly tightened just at the thought of his damn name.

Why, why, *why* did it have to be Sawyer?

Although it didn't take a rocket scientist to understand why, of all the civil engineers on the state's payroll, Sawyer would be the one chosen to take over for the departing engineer. It was the same reason the management team at Bolt-Myer had tasked her with this project. They were both familiar with the area. Like her, Sawyer had grown up in Gauthier. He knew the lay of the land, and, even more importantly, he knew the people. The people in Gauthier could trust that both she and Sawyer would give their all to this project.

Still, if given the option, would she trade her car instead of working with Sawyer? Heck yes, she would.

She'd tried to convince herself that it wasn't a big deal, but the thought of facing Sawyer tomorrow had her stomach in knots. She hated it, but Paxton couldn't deny it. She was human, after all. She had an exceedingly acceptable reason for why just the thought of working with Sawyer made her nervous and uncomfortable and ready to bury her head in the sand and not come out until this project was over.

But she couldn't do that, either.

Nor could she walk into that office tomorrow with even a hint of trepidation or intimidation at seeing Sawyer Robertson for the first time in three years. She'd made her bed where he was concerned—literally. And now it was time to lay in it.

No. No. No! There would be no lying in bed with

Sawyer. It was bad enough they had to share the same work space for the next four weeks. She didn't want to be anywhere near a bed when Sawyer was around.

Okay, so that was a lie, but she was prepared to tell herself whatever was necessary to get through these next four weeks with her sanity intact.

Four weeks! Good God, how would she survive being confined to a tiny conference room with that man for an entire month?

She clutched her stomach with one hand in an attempt to combat the anxiety rioting through her belly. She'd faced some tough challenges in her thirty-seven years, but Paxton had a feeling this would be one of the toughest yet.

"Fine, you win."

Sawyer Robertson tossed the package of fancy adhesive strips on the table and looked around for some good old-fashioned Scotch tape. Detesting the thought of admitting defeat, he quickly picked up the adhesive strips again, his fingers aching from the strain of twisting the heavy cardboard and plastic back and forth.

He dropped his head back and sighed. "Scissors, you idiot."

Shaking his head at his own stupidity, he walked out of the Gauthier Law Firm's small conference room and over to office manager Carmen Mitchell's desk.

"Hey, Carmen, can I borrow a pair of scissors?" Sawyer asked. "I swear they don't want you to get into this thing."

"Give me that," Carmen said. She plucked the package from his hands, poked a hole in the cardboard with a letter opener and sliced it open, then handed it to him.

She snorted, shaking her head. "And to think you were considered one of the smart ones."

Sawyer couldn't help but laugh. He'd attended Gauthier High School with the law practice's longtime secretary. Nice to see she was as smart-mouthed as ever.

"Trust me. Advanced calculus is ten times easier than opening this package," Sawyer said.

"Yeah, yeah, yeah." Carmen waved him off. She motioned to the small table in the corner that held a coffeepot. "There's fresh coffee over there, but it's decaf."

"In other words, there's fresh brown water over there."

"You sound like Matt," she said. "And just like I tell him, you can buy one of those nice single-serve coffee machines with the individual coffee pods, or you drink what I make."

"Or I can just walk across the street to the Jazzy Bean for my caffeine fix," Sawyer said.

"That, too. But I still want the fancy coffeemaker." She looked up from her computer and nodded in the direction of the conference room. "You need any help setting up in there?"

"No, thanks. I've got it from here." Sawyer turned back toward the conference room but then pivoted on his heel. "Hey, Carmen. The project manager should have been here already. Can you point him to the conference room whenever he gets in?"

"Sure, but you know the project manager is—" The phone rang. Carmen held up a finger. "Gauthier Law Firm."

Sawyer held up the pack of adhesive strips and mouthed, "Thanks again," before returning to the conference room and closing the door behind him so that he wouldn't disturb Carmen any more than he already had this morning.

The room was on the smallish side. An eight-foot well-worn, but polished, wooden table took up a vast majority of the space. There were two makeshift desks on either side of the room—small folding tables, each with a table lamp and a chair. A two-drawer filing cabinet stood next to the table on the opposite end of the room from the one he'd chosen. His desk sat underneath a window overlooking Heritage Park.

It was one of the perks of being the first to arrive. If P. Jones wanted a say in which desk he would work at for the next four weeks, he should have shown up for work on time.

Someone, probably Carmen, had placed a yellow legal pad, a pack of pens and a box of paper clips on each desk. All in all it was pretty bare-bones, but that wouldn't last for long. If the past projects he'd worked on were any indication, by the end of the week every surface in this room would be covered with modeling charts, cost estimates and reams of paper covered in specs.

Sawyer unrolled the preliminary diagram of the flood control structure that had been proposed by Bolt-Myer Engineering, the Arkansas-based firm that had won the bid for this project. The company was smart enough to have several Louisiana branches; the state legislature was known for awarding contracts to local companies.

Using the adhesive strips, he tacked the design up to the conference room's paneled walls.

"Much better," Sawyer said as he gave each twenty-four-by-thirty-six-inch printout a cursory glance. He would still need at least another day or so to pore over all the documents he'd received from his supervisor at the Army Corps of Engineers, where he'd worked since returning to Louisiana seven months ago.

He had only been assigned to this project this past Thursday, after his former colleague, Raymond Burrell, abruptly left for a more lucrative position in the private sector. Sawyer couldn't really blame the guy. Ray had a wife and three kids; he had to do what he had to do in order to provide for his family.

Sawyer had missed Friday's kickoff meeting with the project manager from Bolt-Myer. He'd flown out to Los Angeles to be with his aunt Lydia who'd celebrated her sixtieth birthday with a party at her new home in Chatsworth. Sawyer knew it was something his father would have wanted him to do, but that wasn't the only reason he'd flown out there to surprise her. Lydia had been somewhat of a surrogate mother to him ever since his own mother had died more than two decades ago, back when he was still in high school.

But now that his family obligations were fulfilled, Sawyer was ready to get to work. He'd wanted on this project from the very beginning, but he'd been too busy finishing the levee surveying study around Lake Pontchartrain. He put his heart and soul into every job he worked on, but this one was different.

This was Gauthier.

Ray's departure had opened the door for Sawyer to work on something that was close to his heart—saving his hometown from potential disaster.

Once he was done hanging the computer-assisted-design drawings on the walls, he went over to his desk, taking a moment to appreciate the brilliant view of Heritage Park. It was just one of the things he'd missed about Gauthier in the three years that he lived in Chicago.

Sawyer tried not to think about that time for a number of reasons, his ill-fated marriage being only one of them. But of the things he regretted during his short stint in Illinois, the awkward farce of a relationship with Angelique wasn't even at the top of the list.

That spot was reserved for another disaster, one that Sawyer would not allow to happen here in Gauthier.

His complacency back in his old job had cost business owners their livelihoods. It cost some people their homes. Some even lost their pets. All because he hadn't spoken up sooner when his gut told him that something wasn't right.

This was his chance to make up for those past mistakes. He would not remain silent this time.

Would it change what happened in Illinois? No. Nothing would make up for what his inability to speak up had caused, but at least he knew better now. He wouldn't allow the catastrophe that had happened on his last project to happen here.

This town—the place where his mother was born and raised, the place his father had quickly adopted as his own—meant too much to him to let anything happen to it. He wasn't doing this just for the people of Gauthier. He was doing it for his mom and dad. He would take care of the town they both loved so much.

He would make sure this P. Jones person understood that from the very beginning. When it came to Gauthier's flood protection system, there would be no cutting corners.

Sawyer checked his watch—the silver Seiko his father had given him as a gift years ago—and cursed underneath his breath. He'd always considered punctuality to be the most telling sign of a professional. Apparently, he wasn't dealing with a professional here.

He sat behind his makeshift desk and lifted the plans for the proposed reservoir; then he heard muffled voices coming from the other side of the conference room door. He recognized Matthew Gauthier's voice. Matt's family had founded the town of Gauthier and had owned this law firm for generations. There was a feminine laugh. Sawyer figured the other voice must belong to Carmen. But then the conference room door opened. And his heart stopped.

Paxton Jones plopped a hand on her hip and said, "Well, hell."

Chapter 2

"Paxton? What are you doing here?"

The shock on Sawyer Robertson's face was laughable. If this were a laughing matter.

It was not. There was nothing even remotely funny about this.

The moment her eyes popped open that morning, Paxton knew she would live to regret not checking her phone to make sure she'd set the alarm. She and Belinda had stayed out at the bar much later than originally planned, getting the last bit of odds and ends done before tonight's reopening. By the time she fell face-first onto her pillow, Paxton could barely move, let alone check the alarm on her phone. When her mother knocked on the door of her childhood bedroom that morning, Paxton discovered that she'd overslept by more than an hour.

To make matters worse, there was only one bathroom

in the single-wide trailer where she'd grown up, and, as per usual, she had to fight Belinda over bathroom time.

Why did she allow her mother to talk her into staying at home instead of at Belle Maison? Not only was the quaint bed-and-breakfast closer to the Gauthier Law Firm, but Bolt-Myer would have footed the bill for it. Instead, Paxton had to make the twenty-minute drive in from Landreaux, which didn't help with getting in to work on time.

Not the best way to make a first impression.

Paxton gestured to Sawyer's desk. "I wanted that table," she said. Then, remembering that she had to share this space with him for the next four weeks, she added in a more amiable tone, "Good morning."

"Good morning," he replied. He stared at her for a moment before his eyes widened. "Wait." He picked up one of the documents from his desk and, pointing at it, said, "*You're* P. Jones?"

"Since birth," Paxton answered.

The combination of bafflement and amusement remained on his face as he tossed the papers back on the tabletop and rose from his chair. It was downright mystifying how this man could make a simple pair of gray slacks and a plain white button-down look so good. The unassuming clothes fit his tall, solid frame to perfection, the sleeves of his shirt folded back at the cuff, giving the barest glimpse of his powerful forearms.

Sliding his hands into his pockets, he sauntered toward her.

Paxton braced herself for the onslaught of longing that never failed to pummel her whenever she was around him.

Breathe through it, girl.

"This is a surprise," Sawyer said, a hint of a smile lifting the corner of his mouth. "I knew you worked for Bolt-Myer, but I never put two and two together. I assumed the *P* stood for Paul or Patrick."

"Oh, wow! Really?" she asked with exaggerated exuberance. "Your 1950s mentality makes me feel all warm and fuzzy inside."

He held his hands up. "The only thing the paperwork had on it was P. Jones, which you have to admit is a pretty common name. But I shouldn't have automatically assumed it was male. If it makes you feel better, I'll burn a couple of bras to make up for it."

She flat-out refused to smile at his quip.

Sawyer crossed his arms over his chest, and for a moment she forgot to breathe. She had a thing for arms, and could remember all too well what it felt like to have his wrapped around her.

He leaned his hip against the larger conference room table. The way the material pulled across his firm thigh made Paxton want to bend over and bite it. She resisted. Barely.

"Now I understand why Bolt-Myer chose to send someone from their Little Rock offices instead of picking a project manager from Baton Rouge," Sawyer said, completely unaware of her vampiric thoughts. "You probably know this area better than anyone in the entire company."

"Hmm." Paxton did her best impersonation of Rodin's *The Thinker*, dipping her head and fitting her fist strategically underneath her chin. "You know, there's actually a chance that they chose me because I'm one of the best project managers they have."

"Come on, Paxton. I apologize, okay?"

"And what are you apologizing for? Assuming I was a guy, or for insinuating that I'm here because it's convenient instead of my skill to get the job done?"

"For both," he said. "Can't you find it in your heart to give me a break?"

"I'll give you a break when you get out of my spot."

She set her briefcase on the larger conference table next to his leg. Which, yes, she still wanted to take a bite out of. *Dammit*.

"How is this your spot?" Sawyer's voice oozed incredulousness. "I was here first."

"No, *I* was here first. I claimed that spot on Friday when Carmen and I set up this conference room."

He looked over his shoulder at the folding table, then turned back to her, one corner of his mouth tipping upward in a self-satisfied grin. "Maybe you should have left a sign on it," he said.

Oh, how she wished she didn't find the smugness on his face attractive as hell. Seriously, who in their right mind was turned on by cockiness?

Anyone who encountered a cocky Sawyer Robertson.

"Just think of how much confusion could have been avoided," he continued. "I would have known that the *P* in P. Jones stood for Paxton. I wouldn't have been surprised with the Queen of the Tardy Slip showing up late on the first day of the job. And I wouldn't have had the opportunity to fall in love with this desk and its perfect view of the park." He leaned forward, as if getting ready to impart a deep, dark secret. "I have to be honest, Pax. It really is the perfect view. You'll be sorry you didn't get here early enough to claim it."

She bit the inside of her mouth to stop herself from smiling. She'd prepared herself for this. She would not allow Sawyer's teasing to throw her off her game. Because Lord knew if any man could fluster her, it was this one.

"Don't call me Pax," she said.

His brow arched. "So, it's like that?"

"Yes, it's like that." she said. She couldn't handle him calling her by her nickname. It brought up too many memories of the numerous times he'd whispered it throughout that night they'd shared three years ago.

Don't think about that, Paxton silently chastised herself.

"And bringing up that Queen of the Tardy Slip thing is just wrong," she said.

She'd earned that title back in high school, when she would routinely show up late for homeroom. Unlike most of her classmates who had the luxury of going to bed at a decent hour on school nights, she was often helping Belinda out at Harlon's. It made her chances of getting to school before that 7:10 a.m. bell nearly impossible.

Her best friend, Shayla Kirkland, used to joke, saying that the snooze button was Paxton's *real* best friend.

"No need to get upset," Sawyer said. "It's just nice to see that you're still living up to your name."

Paxton let out an aggravated sigh. "Why did Ray Burrell have to quit?"

He slapped a hand to his chest, his dark brown eyes wounded. "I'll try to pretend that doesn't hurt."

She gave him some serious side-eye action before walking over to the other desk, the one that faced a wall. A *wall*. Why hadn't she set her alarm?

Sawyer followed her. *Great*.

He assumed the position he'd taken on the other side

of the long conference table, crossing his arms over his chest and perching himself on the edge of it.

"Why didn't you tell me that you were the project manager?" Sawyer asked.

"When would I have gotten the chance to tell you? I only came into town a few days ago. Besides, I didn't think I had to. I figured you would have run across it while you were reviewing the information you were given when they transferred you to this project."

"I haven't had much time to review the materials. I was out of town this weekend. A family thing."

"That's what I was told during the meeting on Friday," she said.

"It was a party for my aunt Lydia," he explained. He paused for a moment before continuing in a slightly lower tone. "I'm not sure if you've heard or not, but I'm no longer married."

Paxton put her hand up. "Not my business."

His head jerked back a bit. "So it really is like that?"

"Look, Sawyer, it's not my business where you spend your free time or who you spend your time with." She moved her briefcase to the desk and turned to him. Mimicking his pose, she crossed her arms over her chest and said, "As long as you understand that between the hours of eight a.m. and five p.m., your time is my time."

He made a production of looking at his watch. "Is that the case even when you come in at eight forty-five?"

She'd placed the ball squarely on the tee for that one.

Doing her best to maintain a calm, professional air, she said, "I apologize for being late. As project manager I should be the one setting the example."

"I was only joking, Pax." She continued to stare at

him. Waiting. "I mean Paxton," he corrected himself with a pinch of annoyance.

"Thank you."

The laugh he huffed out was devoid of all humor, but Paxton would not allow it to affect her. The only way she would get through these next four weeks with her sanity intact was if she stayed within the boundaries she'd laid out in her head the minute she had learned Sawyer would be replacing Ray Burrell as the state's civil engineer on this project. Allowing Sawyer to speak to her in such familiar terms crossed those boundaries.

"I'm just trying to be professional here," she explained.

"Yeah, I get it," he said, pushing himself up from the table. The traces of humor that had colored his voice earlier were nowhere to be found. "I would, however, appreciate a call if you know you're running late. Just, you know, as a *professional* courtesy."

Paxton acknowledged the slight sting from his words. She guessed she deserved that.

"I agree," she said. "But I don't have your number."

The moment the words left her mouth the mood in the room shifted. Sawyer's gaze caught hers and held. Her admission was almost laughable, considering their history. She had knowledge of his body in the most primitive, elemental way, yet she didn't even know his phone number.

"I guess that's something we'll have to rectify," Sawyer said.

"Yes." She cleared her throat. Nodded. "I'll need your number in case I need to get in touch with you about something for the project."

His gaze remained on her. Probing. Penetrating. It took everything she had within her not to squirm.

One brow peaked over his dark brown eyes. "Is that the only reason?"

"Yes," Paxton said. "That is the *only* reason I will need your number."

He released another of those irritated breaths, running a hand down his face before assaulting her once again with that intense stare.

"Trying to pretend it didn't happen doesn't erase the fact that it did, Paxton. You know that, don't you?"

The subtle drop in pitch of his already decadently deep voice caused a million butterflies to take flight in her belly. Her body reacted to the mere memory of hearing that voice. She could still feel it on her skin, the goose bumps that rose as he whispered the sexiest words imaginable into her ear as his body slowly entered hers.

Paxton sucked in a deep breath. She could not do this to herself. Would not.

There was too much at stake to get distracted by Sawyer and his seductive voice, or the subtle dip in his chin that begged for her tongue to lick at it, or those deep brown bedroom eyes that saw too much. She needed to remain focused. She had a coworker back in Little Rock who tried to show her up every chance he got. Clay Ridgely was on a mission to take Paxton's spot as the leading project manager, and she'd be damned if she let him do it.

That's why she was determined to ignore the hormones spinning around inside her. She had too much riding on this project to allow anything to get in the way of it, especially an out-of-control libido.

With a will she didn't realize she possessed, Paxton

reined in her body's reaction to him and focused on the myriad reasons why it was important they keep things strictly professional.

"It's obvious I will have to set some ground rules on how things will work over these next four weeks," she said.

"Ground rules?"

"Yes," Paxton answered. "We are here to do a job, and that's the only thing I plan to discuss while we're here. This conference room is small enough. We don't have any room for our personal lives to invade it. Are we clear?"

"No," he said.

Her head jerked back. "Excuse me?"

"I disagree. I think it would be better for both of us if we tackled this issue head-on instead of allowing it to hover over us." He shrugged. "Like you said, this place is small. We don't have room for that eight-hundred-pound gorilla you refuse to talk about."

Just the knowledge that they were both thinking about those hours they spent together caused a tingling sensation to travel up and down her back.

This would be a long four weeks.

But she would get through it. There was no way she would allow that one ridiculously delicious indiscretion she'd succumbed to one night several years ago to derail her plans.

"I'm here to do a job, Sawyer," Paxton repeated. "And so are you. Unless it has something to do with this project, I have no intentions of discussing it. End of story." She straightened her spine and lifted her chin just a touch. "Now, I'll ask you again. Are we clear?"

His eyes bored into hers with an intensity that made

her breathless. Finally, thankfully, he relented. Hunching his shoulders, he said, "Fine. You're the boss."

Those words, coming from *his* mouth, set off a different reaction within her, one of pride.

She was the boss. *Her*. Little Paxton Jones from the wrong side of Landreaux Creek.

What she wouldn't give to go back in time, to return to that reticent, unsure girl she was twenty years ago. The girl who'd secretly longed for the man standing across from her, just as every other girl had. Back when he was the star quarterback, student body president and the most handsome human being to grace the hallways of Gauthier High School.

Paxton wondered what that girl's reaction would be if she told her that she would one day be the boss of Sawyer Robertson. Her teenage self would likely laugh and give her a snide *get real* sneer.

But that's okay. Because *this* Paxton knew better.

"Good," she said to Sawyer with a curt nod. "Now that we've established that, would you please consider switching desks with me? I really want that spot by the window."

"I don't think so," he said. "It's only fair that I get to keep it. If you knew you wanted a certain desk, you should have gotten here early enough to claim it."

She stopped just short of growling, but Paxton decided not to push him on it. This was a battle not worth fighting. In fact, it was probably for the best. Without the beautiful view of Heritage Park to distract her she would be more inclined to keep her head down and work harder. This phase of the flood protection project was slated to last for four weeks, but the quicker they worked, the quicker it would be over.

And the quicker she could get away from all this temptation.

As she went about setting her things out on the table that sat underneath a portrait of an old patriarch of the Gauthier family, Paxton laid out the ground rules.

"My team at Bolt-Myer has spent the past six months designing the initial concept package. The next four weeks are basically a state-required bridge between the concept proposal and the design phase, with an out-of-town trip to tour another flood protection system scheduled toward the end of this phase.

"A detailed report of the ICP has been at the courthouse for residents to review since mid-September. The only thing we have to do is present it at the stakeholders' meeting in a few weeks and address resident concerns, review whatever questions have been posted to the website we set up for public input and finalize the preliminary implementation plan."

"You don't have to explain, Paxton. This isn't my first rodeo. I've worked on enough public–private partnerships to know how this works."

She turned and faced him. "Well, I just want to make sure you understand how a project that *I'm* managing works. We have a timetable that we need to stick to in order to get this done on time, and I intend to adhere to it. Are you on board with that?"

He nodded. "I am."

"Good, then let's get to work."

It had been nearly four hours since Paxton arrived at the office, but it had taken Sawyer less than twenty minutes to get a clear picture of what the next four weeks would be like for him.

Pure. Unmitigated. Torture.

Even though she sat on the opposite side of the conference room, he was acutely aware of her every move. Every key she hit on her computer, every time she moved her chair the barest inch, every second she took a damn breath. He felt it all. And it was both intoxicating and agonizing.

His body was still suffering the effects of the jolt it had received when she'd walked through the conference room door, her slim black skirt gently hugging her delicately curved hips. The impact of staring into those rich hazel eyes again hit him with the force of a tornado. Her hair was shorter than it was the last time he'd seen her. The pixie cut made her cheekbones even more pronounced. She was the entire package: beauty, brains and just enough sass to drive him wild.

His aunt Lydia would say this was his just due for making a sexist assumption that he would be working with a male, but in all fairness, most people would have done the same. Construction, especially on this level, was still a pretty male-dominated arena. It hadn't even occurred to him to ask the full name of the project manager listed at the top of most of the documents simply as P. Jones.

Sawyer wondered, just for a moment, what he would have done if he *had* known that the *P* stood for Paxton. Would he have tried to come up with an excuse when his supervisor at the Army Corps assigned him to this project last week?

No, he wouldn't have made excuses. He had never been the type to run.

She had been the one who ran away.

Sawyer tipped his head back and closed his eyes

against the hurt that still pierced his chest whenever he thought about that morning when he'd woken to find her gone.

It had been three years since that night the two of them had ended up in bed together, turning one of the most harrowing days of his life into one of the most memorable. Sawyer could still recall to the minute detail how it felt when he held her in his arms, contemplating the start of something new and wonderful with the girl he'd had a thing for since their days together at Gauthier High School.

Unfortunately, Paxton hadn't felt the same way. She'd slipped out of his bed in the wee hours of the morning, and when Sawyer had finally caught up to her days later, she'd apologized to him.

Apologized, for goodness' sake.

He could still see the regret in her eyes as she told him that they shouldn't have slept together. She then avoided him like he was something filthy on the bottom of her shoe.

And now, three years later, she didn't even want to discuss it.

Bullshit.

Oh, they *were* going to discuss that night, along with her disappearing act that followed the morning after. Sawyer would give her a day, maybe two, but there was no way in hell he could work this closely with her for the next month with all these questions still lingering between them. He deserved some answers, and he planned to get them sooner rather than later.

They worked in their separate corners for most of the morning, staying out of each other's way. Sawyer was encouraged by the fact that once he made the concerted effort to focus, he was able to put thoughts of her out of his head and actually pay attention to the work in front of him.

His stomach's low growl reminded him that they had yet to stop for lunch. He looked down at his watch, surprised to see that it was nearly one o'clock. Just as he turned to ask Paxton what she planned to do for lunch, there was a knock at the door. Carmen poked her head in.

"Hey, guys, not sure if you ate already, but Matt's meeting with the parish council just ended and there are leftover sandwiches, potato salad and sweet tea from Catering by Kiera if you want any."

"That sounds perfect," Paxton said. "I didn't have time to pack a lunch this morning." She turned to him and pointed a finger. "No comments from you."

Sawyer held his hands up. "I didn't say anything, Queen Tardy."

"Queen of the Tardy Slip," Carmen said with a laugh. "I remember that!"

Paxton rolled her eyes at them both. Who knew it would be so much fun to tease her?

Carmen returned a minute later with a small platter of sandwiches on croissants, a pint of potato salad, two bags of chips and a half-gallon jug of tea, along with paper plates, forks and plastic cups. She set it all in the center of the still-empty conference table and backed out of the room.

Paxton took a seat at the table. "Do you mind this being a working lunch?" she asked him. "Jeffery Melber, the lead engineer on the project, just sent me an updated material's list. We can go over it while we eat."

"That's fine," Sawyer said. "I'd made some changes

of my own to the old one. Let me print you out a copy, and we can get to work."

Ten minutes later, Sawyer was positive that she was going to demand a new engineer be put on this job.

"You cannot be serious about this line item," Paxton said, pointing to the titanium valves he'd added to the list, replacing the fortified aluminum valves that had been suggested by Bolt-Myer.

"The titanium valves are of much better quality."

"They're thirty thousand dollars each," she said. Her arched eyebrows formed perfect peaks over her wide eyes. "That's four times as much as we budgeted."

"But they'll last much longer than the aluminum valves. It may be more money up front, but we can make the case to get the better valves because of what it will save in the long run. You'll have to replace all of those aluminum valves in thirty years. The titanium can last for twice as long with proper maintenance."

"It's not going to happen, Sawyer. The fortified aluminum has been through rigorous testing. They exceed the state regulations."

"These are better." He stabbed the materials list with his finger. He refused to budge on this. "Look, Paxton, I've seen what happens when corners are cut to save a few dollars here and there. It turns out costing more in the long run. Why not just build it with the best now and avoid headaches down the road? Not just headaches, but it could prevent something catastrophic from happening."

"Now you're just fearmongering," she said. "The budget does not have room to spend over a million dollars just on valves." She dusted the flaky crumbs of her croissant from her fingers and pressed a napkin to the sides of her mouth. "I understand that someone like you isn't used to worrying about pesky little things like staying within budget, but for those of us in the real world it is a necessity."

That was a cheap shot, and it hit its mark.

Sawyer tossed the pen on the table and sat back in his seat. He folded his hands over his chest and studied her. "So you're going to go there? Really?"

"The truth isn't always comfortable to hear, but it doesn't make it any less true." Paxton said. She straightened her slim shoulders, lifting her chin slightly as she stared him down. "There is no blank check for this project. I was given a specific budget, and I intend to adhere to it, which means you will have to work within it, too, as hard as that may be for someone like you."

Sawyer had not imagined the sneer in her voice when she said "someone like you."

It didn't take a degree in rocket science to uncover the true meaning behind her words or the tone in which she'd spoken. Paxton Jones resented that he had been a rich kid; she always had. As if it was his fault that his father owned the lumber mill that employed a good number of the laborers in town.

The fact that she grew up in Landreaux, one of the poorest areas of Gauthier, did not help the situation. Differences in status or class had never been a huge issue in this town, mainly because other than his family and the Gauthiers themselves, most of its residents were hardworking, lower-middle-class folks. There were those who fell below the poverty line, but instead of deriding them, the people here quietly did what they could to help.

Paxton, however, had never accepted help easily. Neither had her mother, even though Belinda Jones had swallowed her pride a time or two when things had become too much for her to handle. Sawyer was positive that Ms. Jones had never told her daughter about the instances when she had availed herself of the financial assistance the Cheryl Ann Robertson Foundation, which his father had set up in his mother's memory years ago, supplied to needy families in Gauthier. Belinda Jones was too proud.

Like mother, like daughter.

As far as Sawyer was concerned, when it came to this project, Paxton could choke on her resentment. Her hang-ups about his money didn't make a lick of difference to him. Making sure this flood protection system was the very best it could be was more important than worrying about the chip on her shoulder.

"I've worked in this field for a long time," Sawyer said, trying like hell to keep the resentment out of *his* voice. "I understand budgets. I also understand what happens when people allow budgets to compromise good design."

"Forget the titanium valves," Paxton said, slicing the tip of her red pen through the line item. "I'll give you these," she said, pointing to the alternative barrier reinforcement he'd suggested. "But keep in mind if we choose to stick with this design, we're going to have to cut corners somewhere else."

"Stop taking such a hard line," Sawyer said. "Budgets get blown all the time. The last three projects I worked on for the state all were over budget by at least 30 percent. The extra money is already figured into the state's budget, because they know the projects will go over."

"Not on *my* projects," she said. "I don't know how you state boys operate, but one of the things that makes me a good project manager with Bolt-Myer is my accuracy for hitting my budgets and my completion date targets. This project in Gauthier will be no different."

"You're determined to make this difficult, aren't you? Are you doing this just to spite me?"

She turned her chair toward him, her face full of haughty indignation. "How much weight does that giant ego add when you step on your bathroom scale in the mornings?"

Sawyer ran both hands down his face. It was a conceited thing to say. It was also unfair. Within the first hour of working with her Sawyer had already determined that she was, above all else, a professional.

He held his hands out to her. "I just don't want everything to turn into a fight, Paxton. I want you to be open to hearing my side of things."

"I am open to hearing your side. This isn't a dictatorship," she said. "As long as you understand that when it comes down to the final decision, it's *my* ass that's on the line. You get to return to your safe government job, but my job security is tied to my performance.

"I have more riding on this project than you can possibly know, Sawyer, and I will not allow anything to interfere with it. Are we clear on that?"

The intensity in her stare matched the seriousness in her voice. He wanted to refute her words, but they were true. He didn't have as much at stake when it came to his job. He would be fine no matter what.

But this wasn't his typical project. His concern superseded his personal well-being. This was about Gauthier.

"We're clear," Sawyer answered. "This isn't just a job to you. I get that. But it isn't just a job to me, either. I don't go into work every day just to collect a paycheck.

As I'm sure you know, I don't need to," he said before she had the chance to throw it in his face. "However, when it comes to this particular project, I am just as invested as you are. The people of Gauthier deserve the best flood protection system we can provide, and as long as I'm the engineer on this project they're going to get it. You need to keep that in mind when you think about your budgets. Now, are you clear about *that*?"

She held her jaw so rigid Sawyer was certain it would shatter. Several long, intense moments passed between them, sending the tension in the small conference room into the stratosphere.

Paxton was the first to break. If she'd waited two seconds longer, he would have beaten her to it.

Dammit. He could not take an entire month of these showdowns. He would go crazy.

"I'm willing to compromise on some issues," she said. "*If* you can prove that they will make a significant difference to the overall effectiveness of the system. You don't get to just throw something out there because it's this cool new technology that you've been dying to use."

It irritated the hell out of him that she would assume that he could be so frivolous, but Sawyer wasn't up for yet another face-off so soon. He was still catching his breath from the last one.

"Fine," he said. "So, are we going with the titanium valves?"

She popped a potato chip in her mouth, dusted off her fingers and said, "No. Next item."

Chapter 3

Paxton pulled into a slanted parking slot two spaces down from the entrance to the Gauthier Law Firm. She grabbed her briefcase from the passenger seat and exited the car. As she rounded her front bumper, she looked up and down Main Street, and stopped short. The cashmere-silver BMW 750i that she secretly coveted—yeah, she'd looked up the base price; it was way out of her budget even before she'd bought Belinda the bar—was not it its usual parking spot.

Had she actually made it here before Sawyer?

Yes!

She was going to switch those desks. She was getting her window seat today, dammit.

Paxton raced into the law office, waving a quick hello to Carmen before heading down the hallway. She opened the conference room door and halted.

Sawyer, who sat at his desk sipping from a paper cup with the Jazzy Bean's logo, was scribbling on a notepad. He looked up at her.

"What are you doing here?" Paxton asked, her shoulders falling in defeat as she shuffled over to her desk with much less enthusiasm.

"Good morning to you, too," he said with a chuckle. "Why are you out of breath? Have you been running?"

"Only from my car to here," she answered. She set her briefcase on her desk, then walked over to his.

He had on his reading glasses, the bronze wire-rimmed ones that looked so good on him it made her want to scream.

"You're early," he said.

It was ten minutes after eight, which meant she was technically late, but since she'd spent the past week coming in after eight-thirty, she *was* early today.

"Where's your car?" Paxton asked.

He handed her a cup of coffee. "The mechanic's shop."

She hadn't noticed the second coffee cup on his desk. Her heart performed a ridiculous flip-flop at his sweet gesture.

"Thank you. And good morning," she added. She took a sip of the slightly cooled coffee. It had just the right amount of cream and sugar, which meant Shayla Kirkland, the owner of the Jazzy Bean, had likely made it herself. Her best friend knew how Paxton preferred her coffee.

"Did you walk here?" she asked him. Paxton made a habit of not listening to gossip—hard to do in this small town, which fed off gossip the way mosquitoes fed off blood—but she'd heard that Sawyer had bought a house on Willow Street, which was less than ten minutes away on foot.

"I could have, but as muggy as it is this morning I was afraid I'd need a shower after I got here. I'm driving my dad's old Buick for the next few days." He grimaced.

"The burgundy one?" She couldn't stop the sharp laugh that escaped. "I don't know how I missed seeing it parked out there."

"Yeah, the burgundy one," Sawyer said. "I hate that car."

"I can't believe it's still running. It has to be over twenty years old."

Paxton could remember Sawyer driving his dad's car during their senior year of high school, which was twenty years ago this year. She'd missed the reunion this past summer, purposely filling in for a coworker on a job in Memphis so she'd have an excuse. If given the choice to revisit her high school years or frolic through a minefield, she would choose the minefield.

"It's twenty-two years old," Sawyer said. "My dad loved that damn thing. He went through four cars after it, but he refused to get rid of the Buick."

"You didn't have a problem with it back in high school," Paxton pointed out.

"I didn't have much of a choice," he said with a laugh.

Sawyer had driven the Buick up until the week following the big state championship game, when his father had surprised him with a brand-new pickup truck as a reward for leading the Lions to victory and being named MVP for the season.

The shiny black truck had been parked in front of the school with a big red bow on the hood. They had all later learned that the truck also counted as Sawyer's birthday, Christmas and graduation presents that year, but it was still a huge deal. There were not many families in Gauthier who could afford to buy their teens brand-new cars. The lucky ones got their parents' hand-me-downs, and were more than grateful for it.

Paxton could still feel the envy flowing through her veins as she boarded the school bus while at least a dozen of her classmates piled into the cab and truck bed of Sawyer's gleaming new ride. She wasn't jealous of his truck. Belinda didn't have a car of her own at the time; Paxton knew there was no way on earth she would get a car while still in high school.

No, it was witnessing the camaraderie between the group of friends who had joined Sawyer to celebrate his new truck that got to her that day. She was so envious of the bond they all shared, including Shayla, who, even though she had been Paxton's best friend, had also been part of the popular crowd.

Until this day Paxton truly believed her greatest feat was convincing everyone that it had not bothered her in the least that she wasn't included in their number. She'd perfected the unaffected loner facade, the girl who was above the hype of belonging to high school cliques or attending dances or being noticed by the most popular boy in school.

She'd pretended she didn't care, but if anyone had bothered to look just a little closer, Paxton knew they would have spotted the longing in her eyes.

She shook off those thoughts. She was no longer that girl, the one who pined for Sawyer to notice her. She'd proven three years ago that she'd grown into the kind of woman who could hold his attention for hours on end, until he collapsed in a heap of pleasure-filled exhaustion.

Paxton breathed her way through the full-body shudder that coursed through her, silently cursing herself for even allowing her mind to go there.

She went back to her desk to start on today's work, welcoming the distraction of pouring over the field inspection notes collected during the Bolt-Myer team's previous visit to the proposed construction site. She soon settled into what had become a familiar routine over the past week.

She'd been both surprised and relieved at how easily she and Sawyer had fallen into their own little bubbles while working together. He'd spent most of the past week catching up on the project, while she'd focused on the hundreds—literally hundreds—of line items on her master to-do list.

The most important bullet on her list was the preparation for the stakeholders' information session. Paxton had taken to calling it a town hall meeting when discussing it with residents, hoping that the less formal title would encourage more people to attend. As with every major project, Bolt-Myer was required to inform the members of the community what would take place over the eight months while the first stage of the three-stage flood protection system was being constructed and to answer any questions residents may have.

Paxton had facilitated a number of meetings like this in the past, but she knew this one would be different. It wasn't as if she had anything to prove to the people in Gauthier, but that didn't stop her from wanting to show them just what the girl who had been raised by a single mother from the wrong side of the creek had made of herself.

She put in her headphones and turned the volume up

on the classical music she preferred to listen to while she worked. She'd become so immersed in reviewing the request for proposals from local subcontractors vying for the various jobs that would have to be filled once construction was under way that she nearly jumped out of her seat when Sawyer tapped her on the shoulder.

"Goodness!" she yelped, clutching a hand to her chest. Paxton jerked the headphones off. "What?"

"I didn't mean to scare you," he said. "I tried calling out to you, but you have that music so loud that I can hear it even with the speakers over your ears."

"You should have said something sooner if it was bothering you," Paxton said.

"It isn't. That's not what I wanted to speak to you about."

Her brow rose.

"I need you to come over to the table," Sawyer said. "I want to show you something."

She didn't like the forbidding she heard in his voice or the frown lines creasing the corners of his mouth. Trepidation skirted along her spine as she rose from her chair and followed him to the other side of the conference room, closer to his desk.

Over the past week the conference table had slowly acquired more and more items. It was now covered with stacks of papers, file folders and blueprints. Several topography maps of the east side of Gauthier, not too far from the elementary and middle school, were stretched across the table, their ends held down with a stapler, the polished rock that usually sat on Sawyer's desk and two empty coffee mugs.

Sawyer pointed to an area not too far from Mount Zion Baptist Church.

"I hope I'm wrong about this," he said. "But if I'm right, it can stop this entire project dead in its tracks."

Standing at the conference table, Sawyer's eyes slid shut for a moment as he soaked in the sensation of his body being so close to Paxton's. Mere inches separated them as they hunched over the topography maps he'd spread across the space. She'd taken off her jacket; the belt cinched at her waist accentuating her small frame. His fingers itched to wrap themselves around her. His gaze traveled up to her delicately curved chin, past her full mouth and those hazel eyes, which were narrowed with determination as she focused on the maps.

Sawyer caught a whiff of the coconut-and-mango lotion she kept on her desk, along with something else he couldn't identify. That intoxicating scent had tortured him in the most pleasurable way this past week. He smelled her in his sleep, invading his dreams.

It had become a test of his will to fight the urge to call out her name as he lay in bed at night, manually relieving himself of the pent-up sexual tension that flooded his body. He failed each and every night. No matter how hard he tried, he couldn't stop himself from uttering her name in that moment when he found his release.

It didn't matter that they'd spent only one night together, or that he'd had a wife and two additional casual love affairs since that one explosive evening he and Paxton had shared. When it was time to conjure a fantasy, she was always the star.

Sawyer studied the column of her neck, his eyes moving hungrily up the delicate expanse of skin. His tongue darted out on its own accord, the need for just a quick taste of her nearly overcoming his common sense.

"So, what's the issue?" she asked, catapulting him out of his fantasy.

Sawyer cleared his throat and took a step back. "What was that?" he asked. Standing this close to her would only lead to trouble.

As if she'd tracked the route his train of thought had taken, she, too, took a step back, putting a bit more distance between them.

"I asked about the issue you're having with this. I don't see anything that can put a kink in the project."

Remembering that he was here to do a job, Sawyer returned his attention to the map. Using a capped pen, he pointed to a spot just left of Landreaux Creek that connected to a bigger tributary of the Pearl River.

"According to this elevation map, this area should be out of the restricted flood zone." He slid several color printouts out from underneath the binder he'd set there earlier. "However, based on these stats from the aftermath of Tropical Storm Lucy, it saw over two feet of water."

Paxton's forehead wrinkled. She pulled her bottom lip between her teeth, and the urge to run his tongue along the glistening seam made a comeback. Sawyer started running linear equations in his head, hoping it would distract him. It didn't.

"Maybe it was just overwhelmed," Paxton said. "I was already in Little Rock by the time Lucy hit, but, according to everything I've heard, it dumped a lot of rain in a very short amount of time. Shayla said she was afraid the Jazzy Bean would get some water, and this part of town never floods."

"Any area can see heavier standing water than usual if enough rain falls on it in a short time," Sawyer said. "But

Lucy was moving at twelve miles an hour. That's not fast, but still a reasonably steady clip. This area shouldn't be vulnerable to that kind of flash flooding, especially with it being this high up." He shook his head. "Something isn't right here. I think these maps may be off."

"These are the maps Bolt-Myer's project engineers used when developing the initial concept package. Trust me, Sawyer—they're accurate."

"How sure are you?"

Her back went ramrod straight. "Excuse me?"

"Look, Paxton, I know as project manager you've had your hands in every aspect of this project, but I also know that there are a lot of things you have to pay attention to with a project of this size. You trust your engineers to take care of certain things. Now, I want to know how sure you are that these maps are accurate, because based on these flood totals, something isn't adding up."

"I think you're jumping to conclusions."

Sawyer crossed his arms over his chest. "How do you explain two feet of water in an area that should see no more than a couple of inches at the most?"

"It's not just the speed of the storm that you have to take into account," she argued. "The river was also still high from all the snow that melted from that previous winter and traveled down from the north. Gauthier doesn't have robust pumping stations like the ones in New Orleans and other big cities, so they're going to get this type of flooding during the perfect storm, even in places that are not flood prone."

"That's the thing," Sawyer said. "This wasn't the perfect storm. Not even close." He rounded the table and moved to a map he'd hung on the wall. He pointed the pen cap at the center of the Gulf of Mexico. "Lucy formed here and lingered over the Gulf for several days before moving north. The eye of the storm followed the Louisiana–Mississippi state line, which means Gauthier wasn't even on the so-called bad side of the storm. In fact, for the most part, it remained in the lower-left quadrant, which is the best-case scenario."

"But Lucy was a slow mover," Paxton countered.

Sawyer shook his head. "That shouldn't matter. If I'm to believe that the elevation in this area is as high as it is on this map, then Lucy could have lingered for another three days without this part of Gauthier seeing even close to the amount of flooding that it saw."

Paxton let out an exasperated sigh. "Bolt-Myer's engineers went over these topography maps, Sawyer. They would have caught discrepancies."

"Everyone makes mistakes," he said. "Even the best of them."

"Including you?" she asked with that haughty lift to her voice.

Sawyer nearly said yes, even him, but he stopped himself just in time. He wasn't there to bare his feelings over the mistake he'd made on his previous job, he was there to make sure it didn't happen again.

"All I'm saying is that this doesn't add up," Sawyer said. "I'm not questioning the professionalism of your team at Bolt-Myer, but I *am* questioning the accuracy of these maps. I know this may put us back as far as your timeline is concerned, but we have to consider bringing in a surveying team to measure some of these areas again. There's a possibility that new maps will have to be drawn up."

"New maps?" Her screech was so high Sawyer was sure every dog within a five-mile radius heard her. Her brows nearly reached her hairline. "Are you insane? Do you know what that would entail?"

"I'm a civil engineer," he pointed out. "Yeah, I think I know a thing or two about what it would entail."

"Well, as a civil engineer you should know that we don't have the time or money in the budget to have completely new topography maps drawn up. It's ridiculous to even suggest it."

Sawyer took a step forward. "You want to know what's ridiculous? Building a flood protection system based on incorrect specs."

"*You're* the one who thinks the specs are incorrect," she said. She took a step toward him, getting in his face. "*My* engineers thought they were fine."

"*Your* engineers are hundreds of miles away! Order the surveyors, Paxton."

"No!" she shouted.

"I've seen what happens when something is built half-assed. And that is *not* happening with this project." Sawyer pointed at his chest. "Not on my watch."

"Excuse me for sounding like a broken record, but I'm the project manager. It's *my* watch."

"Dammit." Sawyer ran both hands down his face. "Stop being so damn stubborn."

"Stop being so pigheaded," she snapped.

"*I'm* being pigheaded. You're the one—"

The conference room door swung opened. "Hey, hey, hey." Matt Gauthier poked his head in the door. "Is a referee needed in here?"

He and Paxton both stared at Matt for several heartbeats before backing away from each other. His eyes met hers again before drifting lower and landing on her chest. It pumped up and down with her quick, shallow breaths. He was so turned on by their fiery exchange that, if not for Matt standing in the doorway, Sawyer would have probably taken her then and there.

Paxton glanced over at Matt. "I'm sorry we disturbed you."

"Hey, I'm all for passionate debate, but I have a conference call starting in a few minutes, and unfortunately the walls in this place are pretty thin."

"We'll keep it down," Sawyer said.

"Thanks. I'm only here for the next hour. After that you can scream as much as you want to," Matt said with a laugh.

"Actually, I can use a break," Paxton said. She ran her hands up and down her arms as if chilled, while his skin burned with the hot tension still pulsing between them.

She cast a quick glance his way. "I'm going across the street to get a bite to eat."

"We're not done talking about this," Sawyer warned.

Her chin rose. "We are for now." She walked over to her desk and grabbed her purse. She then walked past him, her murmured, "Excuse me," barely audible.

Sawyer braced his hands on the table and dropped his head as all the fight drained out of him. He felt a strong hand clamp him on the shoulder.

"Rough start?" Matt asked.

"You don't know the half of it," Sawyer answered. He blew out a deep breath, dragging a hand down his face.

"Just stick with it," Matt said. "Gauthier needs this. You weren't here for the flooding last year. It was bad, Sawyer. I've never seen that kind of damage before, not even after Hurricane Katrina. We have to make sure it doesn't happen again."

"It won't," Sawyer said. Standing up straight, he

turned and stared Matt directly in the eyes. "I won't get a good night's rest until I'm certain Gauthier never has to endure what it went through with that tropical storm."

Sawyer knew that in order to make good on his promise he would have to figure out why so many places outside the purported flood zones took on so much water. His gut told him that he was on the right track with questioning those maps. All he had to do was convince Paxton that she should listen to his gut, too.

Chapter 4

Sawyer waited at the curb for an antiquated Dodge with a loud muffler to pass before making his way to the other side of Main Street. A quick glance inside the Jazzy Bean's large windows showed him just how packed the coffeehouse and café was. Even though today kicked off the weeklong festivities surrounding Gauthier High School's Spirit Week, which culminated with the homecoming game on Friday, Sawyer knew from experience that it had nothing to do with the crowd at the Jazzy Bean. This was a typical Monday for Gauthier's hottest new eatery.

Since his return from Chicago a little more than seven months ago, Sawyer had been both stunned and encouraged by the changes in his hometown. A lot of the credit went to the discovery of a small back room at the Gauthier Law Firm, which turned out to be an actual stop on the Underground Railroad. Its finding had turned Gauthier into a tourist destination for history buffs. That discovery had been the impetus the town needed to jump-start its growth.

Some were reluctant to allow Gauthier to grow too much, which Sawyer completely understood. The home-grown businesses were a part of what made this town so unique, but change was necessary if the mom-and-pop shops on Main Street were going to survive the massive expansion taking place just twenty minutes west in Maplesville. It seemed as if the business owners in Gauthier had struck just the right balance in encouraging growth while maintaining the small-town charm that was the hallmark of this town.

The Jazzy Bean was one such establishment. The quaint coffee shop and café drew a wide variety of patrons. From men and women in business suits who drove in from the accounting firm in Maplesville, to nurses in scrubs from the clinic on Collins Street, to men in hard hats who worked at his family's lumber mill.

Even though Sawyer didn't have much to do with the operations side of the lumber mill, he knew many of the workers by name. Most of them had worked there for much of their adult lives. There were now a number of second-generation workers, the sons and daughters of men and women who had been loyal to the company his father had founded more than thirty years ago.

Sawyer stopped to say hello to a few of them, and he was quickly sucked into a conversation about the new safety incentive program the current manager had instituted. The safety incentive had been the one idea Sawyer had pitched at the last board meeting. He was happy to hear that it was so well received by the mill workers.

He found Paxton standing at the counter and had to stop just a moment to appreciate the sheer exquisiteness of the way her clothes hugged her trim frame. She was talking to Shayla Kirkland. No, she was a Wright now. Shayla had married the town's new local doctor just before their class reunion this summer.

He and Shayla had shared a bunch of mutual friends back in high school, but Sawyer could never figure out a way to cross that bridge with Paxton, regardless of how hard he tried. And he'd tried everything he could think of in high school to get her to see him as someone actually worth seeing. Nothing had worked.

"Hi, Sawyer," Shayla greeted him.

Paxton looked over her shoulder and sighed. "Can I please have just a moment's peace before you start hounding me again?"

"I'm not hounding you," Sawyer said. "I'm trying to get you to see my side of things."

She took the glass Shayla handed her and walked over to the station with the coffee fixings. Sawyer followed her.

Okay, so maybe he was hounding her. But he had a good reason this time.

"Look," Paxton started before he could speak. "I understand your need to want everything to meet this perfect gold standard that you're used to operating with, but again, you're not taking my budget into consideration. I have to balance what's going to work for this project against how much it will cost. Everything will not be perfect because we cannot afford perfection. It will, however, be sufficient.

"And," she continued after a breath. "Just because it's not perfect doesn't mean we're half-assing anything. I would never shortchange Gauthier. I'm as invested in this town as you are. More so, in fact."

Sawyer's head snapped back, his eyes narrowing. "Wait. *More* so?"

"Yes." She nodded. "My mother's livelihood is here."

"And that automatically means you care more about Gauthier than I do? Give me a break, Paxton. This is my hometown, too. I care about this place just as much as you do."

She let out another of those sighs; the kind that said she was tired of dealing with the insufferable human being standing before her.

"I don't have time to fight with you right now." She grabbed her glass of iced tea and returned to the counter. "Can I see the new menu?" she called to Shayla. "I want to grab some lunch and get back to working on the agenda for the town hall meeting."

"When is it?" Shayla asked, handing Paxton a laminated menu.

"A week from today. I'd really appreciate it if you would get the word out," Paxton said. "This is the community's chance to bring up any questions regarding the new flood protection system before construction begins. I know people have questions."

"You're right about that," someone said.

They all turned as Nathan Robottom, who owned the hardware store several storefronts down on Main, butted into their conversation. He, along with Harold Porter, sat at Shayla's counter, his knobby fingers wrapped around a ceramic mug.

Nathan scooted off his stool and came to where they were all standing. "That new millage tax we approved is supposed to pay for this new levee you guys are putting together, right?"

"Actually," Sawyer started. "It's a combination barrier and reservoir system, but alternatives are still—"

"Yes, it is, Mr. Robottom," Paxton said, cutting him off. "The residents of Gauthier did a good thing when they voted to approve the new tax. We're going to make sure the money is well spent."

She peered at Sawyer over the rim of her coffee cup, her brow pitched high. Sawyer had worked on enough of these projects to understand her body language. Keep things vague for now. If they got too specific this early into the project, everyone with an opinion would be pounding down the doors of the conference room, wanting their ideas on the best way to fix Gauthier's flood problem to be heard.

"Yes, the money will be put to good use," Sawyer said. "We're not going to have another incident like the one that happened with Tropical Storm Lucy."

"Good, because that storm didn't do nobody no favors," Mr. Robottom said as he climbed back onto the stool he seemed to occupy every single time Sawyer came into the Jazzy Bean. "You'll see me at that town hall meeting. I want to make sure it's all on the up-and-up."

"Be there next Monday," Paxton said.

She looked at Sawyer again, a knowing smile playing at her lips, a glimmer of relief reflecting in her eyes. That brief taste of shared camaraderie sank into his bones. Maybe now she could look at them as being on the same team instead of constant adversaries.

Sawyer scored yet another victory when he was able to convince her to eat at the coffee shop instead of bringing their meals back to the conference room. They gave Shayla their food orders, then carried their sweet iced tea to one of the sidewalk tables in front of the Jazzy Bean. They were the only tables available on this busy Monday afternoon.

Sawyer pulled out Paxton's chair without even thinking about it. She stared at the chair for a moment, and Sawyer prepared himself for another lecture on sexism. But she simply said, "Thank you," before taking a seat.

He rounded the small table and sat across from her.

Paxton gazed out over the street, idly stirring the straw poking out of her iced tea. "It's a pretty day," she said.

"Yeah," Sawyer agreed. He looked up at the cloudless sky. "Maybe we'll finally have a day without rain."

"At least the rain showers haven't been too heavy."

He huffed out a laugh. "Are we really talking about the weather?"

She brought her gaze to his. "It seems like the safest topic. Anything else will probably turn into a fight."

Sawyer's eyes slid shut. He tipped his head back and released an aggravated sigh. "It doesn't have to be that way, Paxton. For the most part last week was peaceful. Why can't we go back to that?"

"You don't get to ask that question, not when you are the one responsible for creating the chaos."

"Okay, first of all, chaos is a bit over the top. I made an observation, a valid one. I refuse to back down when it comes to the surveyors. You need to trust me on this one, Paxton. The very least you can do is consult with the engineering team at Bolt-Myer. Let them know my concerns and see what they think."

She sat upright in her chair. "I—"

"Okay, here we go," Shayla said, arriving at their tables with her hands full. She set the first plate in front of Sawyer. "One caprese with extra basil." She turned to Paxton. "And one roast beef po'boy with a bag of chips. I'm out of those butter pickles you love so much," she said. "I forgot to order additional jars from Mrs. Blackwell before she went out of town. I'll give you two spears the next time you're here."

Shayla's eyes darted between Paxton and Sawyer. "Um, is everything okay?" she asked.

"It's fine."

"Yes."

"I totally believe you both," Shayla drawled. "And I just won the Publishers Clearing House Sweepstakes. That blue van should pull up any minute now."

"Shayla, please just leave it alone," Paxton told her. "I'll talk to you later."

"Fine," Shayla said, giving Paxton a look that implied that they would certainly talk later. Maybe once Shayla got the full story about whatever was going on, she could clue Sawyer in. Just like old times.

He'd never admitted to Shayla how he felt about her best friend back when they were in high school, but Sawyer had always seen her as an ally. She was smart, and unlike Paxton, who had never been able to see past that giant chip on her shoulder, he knew that Shayla could tell that his interest had been real.

She probably thought he was pathetic as hell to still seek out Paxton's attention after all these years, especially if she knew about that night he and Paxton had spent together, and how she had subsequently left him without a word. She had to know about their one-night stand. Girls talked. Especially girlfriends who were as tight as Shayla and Paxton.

Maybe if he could convince Shayla to petition her on his behalf, maybe then he could convince Paxton to look beyond that image of him that she'd created in her own mind—a spoiled rich guy. Something he'd never been in his life. Sure, his family had money, but Sawyer had never flaunted it. His parents had raised him to be more humble than that.

Paxton's image of him was of her own making. Maybe if she took the time to really *see* him—the *real* him—she would like what she saw.

Or maybe he was just kidding himself.

After all, they weren't in high school anymore. He couldn't rely on Shayla to help him win the girl.

But he had to do *some*thing. Sawyer refused to believe all was lost. He knew Paxton felt something for him—something other than scorn, or even worse, indifference. He'd felt it that night; he saw it even now when she looked at him. Those times when she forgot to raise her guard, when she allowed that shield to fall and gave him a glimpse of her softer, sweeter side. That's when he knew that she was worth the fight.

"Paxton—" he started, but she cut him off.

"Can we just not talk about work right now?" she said. "I don't want to argue."

"And you think I do?"

She looked at him. "No, I know you don't. It's just… easier."

"It's easier to argue with me?"

She studied him. "Yes," she said. "I know it isn't fair, but…" Her voice trailed off as she shrugged and reached for her tea. She took the lemon wedge and shook off the excess tea before sticking it between her lips and sucking.

Sawyer was hit with a tidal wave of longing so strong he nearly drowned. He was broadsided with memories of the last time he'd witnessed her do that very thing.

It was the night he'd walked into Harlon's bar, hoping to find refuge from one of the shittiest days of his life at the bottom of a shot glass. It had been the second time in his life that Sawyer had entered the bar. Hell, he could probably count the number of times he'd driven out to Landreaux on one hand.

But that night he had needed solace and solitude, so he'd made the drive across the creek, because he figured no one would bother him. He hadn't counted on seeing Paxton there, because by that time he'd come to terms with the idea of there never being anything between him and the girl he'd pined for throughout his adolescence. In fact, Sawyer had forgotten that she occasionally still worked at the bar.

She must have sensed his pain that night, because instead of ignoring him, she'd made a point to check in on him several times. And when he'd begged her to not let him drink alone, she'd broken her own rule of drinking while on the job, poured herself a shot of tequila and sucked hard on a lemon after downing it.

Sawyer's eyes zeroed in on her mouth as she sat across from him right now, and his body ached as he remembered the magic those lips had worked on him later that night. The way she'd trailed her delicious tongue along his body, and how he had reciprocated in kind, licking his way up and down her smooth skin, sweetly tasting every inch of her.

"Don't look at me like that," she said. "Stop... remembering."

He knew he wasn't the only one affected. He *knew* it.

"How many times this past week have you thought about that night?" Sawyer asked her.

"I haven't."

"Liar."

She tossed the lemon wedge onto her plate. "It's this damn lemon," she said. "You weren't thinking about that night until I sucked on it."

"That's where you're wrong, Pax. I can't tell you how many times I've thought about it—not just this past week, but for the past three years."

Disbelief was evident in the look she tossed his way.

"Are you saying that you haven't thought about it the last three years?" he asked her. She remained silent, but he caught the stiffening of her jaw.

Sawyer huffed out a gruff laugh. Shaking his head, he said, "Telling yourself that you're not affected doesn't make it true, Paxton. It's just a form of lying to yourself."

She tore her eyes from his, choosing instead to stare at the building across the street. "Sometimes lying to yourself is a good thing," she said. "It's self-preservation."

"So you'd rather lie to yourself than face the truth of what happened between us? Do you really think it's realistic to ignore it?"

Frustration saturated the heavy sigh she blew out. She returned her eyes to his, a mixture of annoyance and pleading resting in their hazel depths. "Sawyer, we've been over this."

"No, we haven't. I've tried to bring it up, but you won't discuss it."

"Because there's nothing to discuss."

"Paxton, we—"

"We spent the night together. *One* night. That's all it was, Sawyer. I'm over it."

It was difficult to ignore the hurt that flashed across Sawyer's face, but Paxton knew it was for the best. Acknowledging that her words had the ability to hurt him would require her to acknowledge that there actually was more than just sex between them, and she wasn't willing to do that.

His strong jaw was rigid with tension, frown lines bracketing his mouth. His stony gaze held a hint of mockery.

"I guess you think I should just get over it, too," he said, his lips tilting in a cynical smile.

"Sawyer—" Paxton started, but she stopped before she could apologize.

This is what she wanted. She wanted him to get over it and not bring up that night ever again. Because while he may have thought it was a night of shared passion, for her it represented something entirely different.

It was one of the most selfish acts she'd ever committed.

She'd used him that night. Selfishly. Unrepentantly.

She had known he was hurting that night. It had been visible on every part of his face. Paxton had been floored to even see him in her part of town. The only people who tended to hang out in Landreaux were the people who lived there. Paxton was hoping that would change when her mother's new and improved bar officially reopened tonight, but realistically there was nothing else in Landreaux to entice people who lived in the southern portion of Gauthier to cross the creek.

But Sawyer had come out to her neck of the woods that night three years ago. He'd told her that he'd just returned from the hospice care facility in Slidell where he had brought his father.

His voice had held so much hurt as he shared that it was the step he had dreaded since the moment the doctors told him his father's cancer was terminal. He'd gone through the same with his mother back when they were in high school, and Paxton remembered that period when his normally smiling face had been drawn and distant. The golden boy had lost a bit of his usual luster.

Like it had for his mother many years prior, moving into hospice care had signaled the final stage for his father.

Paxton had taken pity on him. How could she not when she could see how much he was hurting?

She'd served him one drink and then another. Then she'd joined him at the end of the bar after he'd begged her to do so. Paxton had promised one quick drink before she had to go back to work, but it had been a slow night at Harlon's, and most of the patrons were regulars who didn't require constant attention.

She and Sawyer had shared a drink, and they'd talked. She'd leaned on the bar and talked to him for more than two hours in an attempt to get his mind off his troubles. Then she'd offered to drive him home, to the huge house he'd grown up in on Elm Street in the heart of Gauthier. A home she used to stare at with longing, wondering what it looked like on the inside.

Once there, Paxton's well-meaning generosity had taken a backseat to her selfishness. Forgetting that she was there to help him, she'd decided to help herself to the one man she'd always longed for.

She'd taken advantage of him that night, preying on his vulnerable state of mind and finally fulfilling her fantasy. It had been everything she'd expected and more, but when she'd awakened the following morning, Paxton had been so ashamed that she could hardly stand to look at herself in the mirror.

All she had to do was reverse their roles to realize how disgusting her actions had been. If it were Belinda she had just taken to hospice care, and Sawyer had used her in that way, she would despise him for it. He just didn't realize that he should feel that same way about her.

As she looked at him across the table right now, Paxton felt a pang of the same guilt she'd felt the morning following their one-night stand. She'd hurt him again with her lie—because God knew she was not over sleeping with him.

Picking up bits of potato chip crumbs from the table with the pad of her finger, she cleared her throat and said, "I'm sorry for snapping at you."

His brow rose. "Did you snap?"

"You know what I mean, Sawyer. I didn't mean to sound so harsh."

He rested his forearm on the table and leaned forward. "You just told me that you're over sleeping with me. Tell me how that wouldn't sound harsh to any man?" he asked, his deep voice edged with tension.

"Sawyer—"

"But here's the thing," he continued. "I don't believe a word of it. You're no more over that night than I am." His voice dropped to panty-melting depths. "You think about it when we're in that conference room together, with nothing but that table separating us."

A rumble of panic coursed through her at the thought

of him seeing past the facade she took such care in main-taining. Paxton steeled herself against the truth of his words and summoned the most cynical look she could muster.

"That ego of yours is astounding," she said with a sneer.

"Cut the crap," Sawyer said. "This has nothing to do with ego." He edged even closer toward her. "I don't believe it when you say you're over that night because I was there, Pax, and I remember every single time you screamed my name. I remember how it felt when you clawed at my back, how you locked your legs around my waist. How your thighs felt against my face."

She squeezed her legs together and tried her hardest not to whimper with the want slowly spreading through her bloodstream.

Sawyer sat back in his chair and lazily twirled his straw around his glass of iced tea.

"I don't care what line you try to feed me. I won't be-lieve it," Sawyer said. "You may regret that it happened, but I'll be damned if you're over it."

Paxton closed her eyes. When she opened them again, he was still staring at her with that look that said he saw right through her.

"I just want to know why you left," he said. "Just tell me why you walked out that morning, and I'll drop it."

Paxton studied her hands for several heartbeats be-fore returning her gaze to his and handing him the lam-est excuse in the world.

"I realized it was a mistake," she said. "Can we please just leave it at that? Please, Sawyer. We have three more weeks of working together. Please don't make this un-comfortable for me."

The intensity in his stare singed her skin, but thankfully he didn't comment further.

A moment later, Shayla showed up at their table balancing a tray on her hip.

"I hope you two are staying for the homecoming parade," she said as she removed their empty plates. "It started at the high school twenty minutes ago. It should reach Main Street in the next five minutes or so. The sheriff will be closing the road soon."

"Oh no." Paxton pushed away from the table. "We need to get back to the other side of the street before it's blocked off."

"Why don't we just stay and watch the parade?" Sawyer said in a deceptively cool voice. "It's not as if either of us will be able to concentrate on work with all the noise anyway."

"He's right," Shayla said.

Yes, he was. And, honestly, Paxton wasn't ready to return to the confines of that tiny conference room with him anytime soon, not with the tension still pulsing between them.

"Stay right where you are," Shayla said. "You two have the best seats in the house."

As if Shayla's statement had heralded it in, the faint sound of drums began to fill the air around them. The patrons who had been eating lunch inside the Jazzy Bean, along with others pouring out of the surrounding businesses, began to line the sidewalk. Moments later, the Gauthier High School marching band's drum major high-stepped her way down the street, her knees nearly reaching her chest.

As people crowded around their table, Paxton and Sawyer both stood.

She chanced a glance his way and found him staring at her.

She sent him a plea with her eyes, silently begging
him to drop the issue of their one-night stand. She
wanted them to return to that companionable atmosphere
they'd discovered over the past seven days.

Paxton's limbs went weak with relief when she saw
the faint accepting smile ghost across his lips.

Thank God.

Paxton turned her focus to the parade, which had finally reached them. It was hard not to be sucked in by
the excitement of it all. The marching band led the way,
dressed in their green-and-white uniforms, their freshly
polished instruments reflecting the brilliant sun that finally shone through the clouds after a week of overcast
skies and off-and-on rain showers.

The dance team and pom-pom squad followed the
band, and in a truck right behind them was the cheer-
leading squad. The double cab was decorated with
garland made out of crepe paper, balloons tied to the
antennae and poster boards proclaiming that the Gauthier Fighting Lions would beat the Maplesville Mustangs
taped to the doors and side panels.

Members of the homecoming court followed the
cheerleaders, each in their own car. Paxton discovered
that the trend these days was to rent fancy convertibles
for the parade. Someone had even rented a bright yellow Lamborghini.

The stars of the homecoming parade were, as always,
the members of the Gauthier High School football team.
Like the cheerleaders, they rode in the back of several
pickup trucks, all wearing their football jerseys sans
shoulder pads.

Nathan Robottom, who stood alongside them, pointed out his grandson, who was a varsity wide receiver and who was already being recruited by several division one colleges in Louisiana and Mississippi.

As she watched the squad toss Mardi Gras beads, candies and Moon Pies to the mass of people now crowding the sidewalks, Paxton waded through an odd sea of annoyed nostalgia.

On one hand she was charmed by this unique slice of small-town living that was the hallmark of places like Gauthier, but standing there, watching the revelry and the reverence paid to the football players and cheerleaders brought her back to her unsettling high school days. When it came to things like homecoming and pep rallies, Paxton had always felt as if she was on the outside looking in.

She glanced over at Sawyer. The smile on his face stretched from one end to the other as he caught a small plush lion that one of the football players had thrown his way. He handed it to Mya Anderson, who had come out of Claudette's Beauty Salon with her two young daughters in tow.

"This must bring back fond memories for you," Paxton said. He looked over at her, his brow raised. "Seeing the football players in all their glory," she clarified. "As I recall, you experienced a fair amount of acclaim back in those days."

"You sound jealous," he said in a teasing tone.

"I am not." She huffed with exaggerated affront, relieved to see them return to a bit of the good-natured banter they'd found over the past week. Paxton shrugged. "Besides, this was never my thing."

Sawyer turned to her. "Why is that?" he asked.

Paxton was caught off guard by the genuine curiosity coming through his steady gaze. "It...it just wasn't," she replied.

"Is it because you were too cool to be bothered with all this silly homecoming stuff, or was there something else?"

"It just wasn't my thing," she repeated. "I never understood the hero worship when it came to football players. Everyone treated them like they were gods. It just made me less interested."

"Because if the rest of the crowd found something interesting, you thought it should be ridiculed. That's how you used to look at things back then, right?"

"Not everything," she said, her eyes still focused on the parade gliding down Main Street. "Just football players."

Several heartbeats passed before he said, "Maybe you should have given the football players a chance back in high school."

Paxton whipped her head around to look at him. She didn't know what to do with the unrestricted honesty staring back at her.

She wanted to ask him what he meant, but he had already returned his attention to the parade. She stood there with her eyes on the trucks that continued to slowly roll along the roadway, but her mind remained on Sawyer's words.

It almost sounded as if he'd had a thing for her back in high school. It was ridiculous to even think that. It may have been twenty years ago, but Paxton could remember those days all too well. Sawyer Robertson hardly noticed her back then. In a school with a little more than three hundred students, in a town that was small enough that everyone knew everyone, she still had never been on his radar.

The whirling sirens of the Gauthier Volunteer Fire Department's red fire engine, also decked out in green-and-white crepe paper, brought her back to the here and now.

As the crowd dispersed, she and Sawyer returned to the conference room. Paxton had already told him that she would leave a bit early today to help Belinda prepare for the grand opening of the River Road Bar and Grille, but there were a couple of things that she needed to finish before she could call it quits for the day.

If only she could concentrate on her work.

She fought the urge to bring up their conversation during the parade. Had he meant that she should have given *all* football players a chance back in high school, in the general sense? Or did he mean one player in particular?

"Shouldn't you be heading out soon?"

Paxton jumped, even though he'd spoken in a normal tone. She looked at the time on her laptop.

"Yeah," she said before putting the machine in sleep mode. "I need to stop in at Shayla's. She has some special grand opening cookies she made for tonight. Not your typical bar fare, but I didn't want to hurt her feelings."

He walked over to her and assumed his favorite position, his arms crossed while he perched on the edge of the larger table.

"Do you all have everything in place for tonight?" he asked.

She nodded, unable to keep the excited smile from creasing her lips. "We're as ready as we can get. Just have to hope people show up."

"They will."

She slipped her laptop inside her briefcase and snapped it closed.

"Paxton?" She looked up at him. "Just because I haven't brought it up again, don't think you're getting away without explaining why you think the night we spent together was a mistake." He pushed away from the table and sauntered to her, his relaxed, languid stride in direct opposition to the intensity in his eyes. "And don't think for a minute that you're going to get away with that sorry-ass excuse you tried to feed me earlier today."

He stopped inches away from her. "You still think about that night. I know you do, Pax. And I'm going to make you admit it."

She managed to take a much-needed breath as she crossed her arms over her chest and stared him down. "Is that a challenge?" she asked.

A smile curved up the corner of Sawyer's mouth. "That's not a challenge, sweetheart. That's a promise."

Paxton entered the Jazzy Bean and, spotting Shayla at the register, walked over to the counter, folded her arms on top of it and dropped her head onto them.

"Let me take a wild guess," Shayla said. "Bad day?"

Paxton's response was a low growl. She lifted her head just enough to peer up at her friend. "You haven't applied for a liquor license, have you?"

"Ah, no," Shayla answered with a laugh. "The best I can do is an iced tea, and not the Long Island kind."

"That'll do," Paxton said. "But hit me with some real sugar instead of the artificial stuff. I deserve it after the day I've had. Are the cookies ready?" Paxton asked.

"They're in the back," Shayla said as she filled a clear

plastic cup with ice and dispensed raspberry tea over it. "They are *so* adorable, if I do say so myself. They're shaped like fleur-de-lis, with *Saints* scrolled across them in gold icing. They're going to be a hit tonight." She handed Paxton her iced tea. "But you can't get the cookies until you tell me about your crappy day. You owe me the story behind that arctic air you and Sawyer brought in here at lunchtime."

Shayla walked over to the small rectangular window that led to the kitchen. "Lucinda," she called to her cook. "I'm going to take twenty minutes."

She and Paxton walked outside to the same table she and Sawyer had occupied earlier.

"I can't stay long," Paxton warned.

"I know," Shayla said. "You need to help Belinda get ready for tonight. I'm sorry I won't be able to make it. I promised Leslie I'd watch the girls. She and Gabriel have tickets for the game."

Kristi and Cassidy Kirkland were Shayla's young nieces—her deceased brother's two adorable children. It was the intention of helping her sister-in-law raise the girls after her younger brother's untimely death that had initially brought Shayla back to Gauthier. Even though her sister-in-law had remarried, Shayla still played a huge part in the girls' lives.

"I'm hoping I'm too busy waiting on customers tonight to notice your absence," Paxton told her.

"You will be. Gauthier takes care of its own. The folks here are going to support your mom." Shayla reached over and grabbed the iced tea she'd poured for Paxton, taking a sip before setting it back on the table. "Now, what has you craving liquor in the afternoon?"

Paxton tipped her head back and released an aggravated sigh.

"A number of things, but this flood protection project tops the list," she lied. Straightening in her seat, she braced her hands on the table. "I prepared myself for mishaps. Everyone knows that it's foolish to go into a job thinking that it will all go as planned, but I hadn't expected such a huge setback so soon."

"What's wrong?"

"Sawyer brought up a potential problem with the topography maps this morning, and I think maybe he's right. If he is, it will throw everything completely off track."

"Is this what you two were arguing about earlier?"

"Which time?" Paxton snorted.

"Pax," Shayla said, admonishment coloring her tone. "Please don't tell me you've been Mean Paxton the entire time you and Sawyer have been working together."

"Excuse me, but who is Mean Paxton?"

"Oh, please. Give that innocent act a rest, girl. I know you. I'll bet you spent all of last week giving Sawyer a hard time, and for no good reason."

"I have not. We've gotten along just fine so far. He's stayed out of my hair and I've stayed out of his. Until today, that is. And I do not have a mean side," Paxton argued.

"You most certainly do have a mean side," Shayla said. "And I don't like the thought of you and Sawyer just 'getting along.' I was hoping there would be some sparks between you two. The good kind of sparks."

Paxton's head reared back. "Sparks?"

"Yes, sparks. You know, those tingly little bursts of

magical feelings that happen when two people realize they would be perfect together?"

Paxton could not stop her jaw from dropping as she stared at her best friend.

She and Shayla had been inseparable since the third grade, when they had bumped into each other in the cafeteria and spilled spaghetti sauce all over their clothes—on school picture day of all days. Instead of getting in a fight, which the classmates who had crowded around them immediately started to chant in favor of, she and Shayla had both laughed at each other. They'd instantly recognized that they were kindred souls.

Throughout their years of schooling and in all the years beyond, Shayla was the first person Paxton called whenever she had news to share, a problem to solve or just time to kill.

But she had never told her best friend about the one-night stand she'd had with Sawyer. In fact, she'd never told Shayla about her true feelings for Sawyer, stretching back to their years in high school. She didn't want to put Shayla in the position of telling her that he was out of her league. Paxton had known that all along.

Yet it suddenly seemed as if Shayla didn't feel that way at all.

"Why would you think there would be magical sparks between me and Sawyer?" Paxton asked her. "I've barely said two words to him since high school," she lied. "In fact, Sawyer and I have never had much to say to each other. I wasn't even on his radar before we started working on this project."

Shayla looked at her as if she were a foreign object underneath a microscope. "Wait—are you seriously still in the dark about this?"

"About what?" she asked, reaching for her iced tea.

"Oh, come *on*, Pax." Shayla groaned. "Seriously? You cannot be this blind. Sawyer has had a thing for you since high school."

"What!" Paxton screeched.

"Just stop it," Shayla said. "I refuse to believe you are this freaking blind."

"You're insane."

"Really? Don't you remember how he used to come over to the animal shelter all the time?"

"He used to come there because you were tutoring him."

"The boy was half-crazy over you, Pax! Think about it," Shayla continued. "Sawyer graduated fifth in our class. He had more academic scholarships than football scholarships. Do you really think he hung around the animal shelter because he needed tutoring?"

"You don't know what you're talking about," Paxton said as she took a sip of tea. Sure, they'd slept together as adults, but there was no way Sawyer Robertson had any kind of thing for her back in high school.

Maybe you should have given the football players a chance...

Paxton sat up straight. "Wait a minute."

"You catching a clue?" Shayla asked.

She had never considered the fact that Sawyer was indeed an excellent student. He was a jock. Jocks were dumb—at least that's what she told herself in those days.

"The entire time he was being 'tutored,'" Shayla said, using air quotes, "he would steal looks at you. He even asked me if you had a date for prom, but you'd already told me that you weren't planning on going."

"Prom?" Paxton asked, her mind still reeling from the

thought of Sawyer coming to the animal shelter where she and Shayla volunteered as teens to see her.

She had been so sure that no one would ask her to the prom—or, even worse, that someone would ask her as a joke or a stupid juvenile bet—that she had declared early on that she would not participate in the silly time-honored tradition. Instead of going to the prom with her classmates, she'd spent that Saturday night as she'd spent most of her Saturday nights back then, hauling ice, slicing lemons and washing glasses at Harlon's. And thinking about all the fun she was missing out on.

Was it possible that she could have spent that night with Sawyer?

Shayla reached across the table and covered her hand. "Do yourself a favor and lock Mean Paxton in the basement for a while. Sawyer is a good guy. You should give him a chance."

Paxton gave her a subtle nod, but she didn't say anything else. Apparently, that was enough for Shayla. She dropped the subject of Sawyer and switched to the lineup of events she had planned for the Jazzy Bean's Friday Night Jazz Night.

As her best friend rattled on, Paxton's mind remained on their previous conversation. That Sawyer felt a certain attraction toward her now was undeniable. She'd managed to convince herself that it was purely physical and based solely on his drunken memories of the few naked hours they'd spent together. But if there was some truth to what she'd gleaned today—first from Sawyer and now from Shayla—there was a possibility that the boy she'd longed for for more than twenty years had felt the same way about her.

It was too unbelievable for Paxton to comprehend.

She made a show of checking the time on her phone and said, "I'm sorry to drink your tea and run. But I need to get to Landreaux."

"And I need to finish up here so I can pick up Kristi and Cassidy," Shayla said as they rose from the table. She pointed a finger at her. "And I'm serious when it comes to Sawyer."

Apparently, the subject had not been forgotten.

"I know you are," Paxton replied. "But it's a moot point until this project is done. I don't mix business with pleasure."

"That's a bald-faced lie. What about that coworker in Little Rock?"

"Believe me, he doesn't count," Paxton said. "You want to help me bring the cookies to my car?"

Shayla followed her into the coffee shop, and together they gathered the bakery boxes filled with sugar cookies to Paxton's car. She opened the rear gate with the remote on her key ring, and they positioned the boxes around the extra suitcases that were still in the back of her SUV.

"You look as if you're living out of your car," Shayla commented.

"Because there's no room at Belinda's. Can you believe she turned my old room into a sewing room? She left the daybed, but everything else? Gone."

"I didn't know she sewed."

"She doesn't, but Judy Monroe was selling all of her sewing supplies. Belinda has never been able to back away from a deal."

"That is hilarious," Shayla said with a laugh. "You know if you're ever at the office late and don't want to drive all the way home you can stay in our guest room."

Paxton held up a hand. "No, thank you. I have no interest in hearing that honeymoon bed knocking against the wall."

"We're past the headboard-banging stage," Shayla said. She tipped her head to the side. "Actually, thinking about last night—"

"Bye." Paxton closed the gate and rounded the back of the SUV.

"Oh, do you want to meet before the game on Friday?" Shayla asked. "We can go together."

"Um, do you remember me ever going to a game back when we actually were in high school?" Paxton asked as she climbed behind the wheel. "Why would I want to go to one now?"

"It's homecoming. You can make an exception this time. And its not as if you've *never* gone to a Lions football game."

Paxton gave her some serious side-eye.

"Okay, you went to *a* game," Shayla said. "But you had fun that night, remember?"

"I fell on my ass while walking up the bleachers, and later that night Scotty Mitchell spilled his beer all over my favorite shirt. I spent the majority of my adolescence working in a bar, but it wasn't until that night that Belinda asked if I'd been drinking."

"Well, Scotty doesn't drink anymore," Shayla said. "Carmen made him give it up after he had that kidney stone."

Paxton's face scrunched up. "Ugh, are we really that old? People we went to high school with are developing kidney stones?"

"I know, right?" Her eyes turned pleading. "Would you at least consider coming to the game on Friday? It'll be fun."

"All depends on your definition of fun," Paxton said. "Thanks for the tea. I'm assuming it was on the house since you didn't ring me up."

"You have a tab which must be paid in full at the end of the month. Unless you move back to Gauthier permanently. Do that, and I'll give you all the free tea you want."

"Nice try." Paxton laughed, waving from behind the wheel as Shayla went back into the coffee shop.

As she was preparing to back out onto Main Street, she looked into her rearview mirror and noticed Sawyer's car still parked in front of the law office. Her breath hitched, and that annoying little flutter she got in her stomach whenever he was around came to life.

Was Shayla telling the whole story when it came to Sawyer's feelings about her back when they were in high school, or was it her friend's starry-eyed newlywed optimism rewriting history? Paxton didn't think she could be so blind as to not recognize that the guy she'd wanted for so long had actually been interested in her.

"Who are you kidding?" she said aloud.

Even if she'd had the barest inkling that Sawyer had had feelings for her back then, she doubted she would have been open-minded enough to accept them.

Some people would have probably labeled her as bitter back in those days, but Paxton thought realistic was a better adjective. She had *always* been an outsider looking in.

She'd wanted to go to dances. She'd wanted to join their clubs and go to slumber parties. She'd even wanted to be a cheerleader, although Paxton would rather walk down Main Street stark naked in the middle of the homecoming parade before she admitted that secret to anyone.

She could still remember practicing in her room when she was home alone. She'd wanted to be a cheerleader because, back then, Sawyer Robertson only dated cheerleaders. She wanted to be the kind of girl that Sawyer would want to have on his arm.

But she wasn't that girl. She had *never* been that girl.

And Shayla actually thought she would put herself through the misery of attending the homecoming game this Friday?

As if!

She could do without any reminders of the Paxton she used to be in high school. She'd rather focus on the Paxton she was today—strong, independent, financially stable—and in no danger of falling for girlhood dreams that were not likely to ever come true.

Chapter 5

Belinda walked up to the bar and tapped twice on the freshly polished surface. "I need two pitchers of Abita Purple Haze," she called.

"Coming up," Paxton returned. She snatched two plastic beer pitchers from under the bar and filled them with the popular local brew. As she set both on a tray and pushed it toward Belinda, Paxton couldn't help but laugh. "Look at you," she said, gesturing to her own mouth. "You think that smile can get any bigger?"

"No," her mother said. She stuck her tongue out at Paxton before carting the pitchers of beer to one of the crowded tables.

They were all having a hard time containing their smiles tonight. Gauthier had turned out in droves to support the official grand opening of the River Road Bar and Grille, although, as she predicted, everyone was still referring to it as Harlon's. She didn't care. Paxton couldn't decide whether to cry tears of joy or break out in her happy dance. She would likely do both before the end of the night, but right now she was so busy she hardly had a chance to breathe.

Donovan, who Paxton had to admit had been a godsend tonight, backed his way out of the kitchen's swinging door, his arms loaded with baskets of hot wings.

"Jessie needs that flour, Pax," he called to her.

Dammit. Paxton snapped her fingers. "Tell her I'm on it," she said.

"On what?" Belinda asked as she squeezed sideways through the tiny opening that led to the back of the bar. The next phase of renovations would include one of those hinged bar flaps.

"I need to run to my car before Jessie has a coronary," Paxton told her. "The extra flour she asked me to pick up is in there. I didn't think we'd need it before the game even started."

"Go on," Belinda said. "I've got this. I don't want anyone having to wait on wings."

Paxton concurred. They needed to keep the clientele happy and fed. Many of the people here could just have easily given their business to the national restaurant chain that had opened in Maplesville several weeks ago. She'd never admit it out loud, but inwardly Paxton had been nervous as hell that the new place would take business away from her mother's, making it a failure before it ever got off the ground.

She never should have doubted the people of Gauthier, especially those from Landreaux.

She ran out to her car, and with Donovan there to help, carried in the fifty-pound sack of flour that would be used to coat the chicken wings that were flying out of the kitchen at a record pace. Once she was sure that everything was under control, both in the kitchen and behind the bar, Paxton went out to clear tables and greet patrons.

As she looked out over the crowd her chest filled with so much pride she thought her fitted River Road Tavern T-shirt would bust at the seams. Pride not only for her mother but for her entire community.

She'd always had a love-hate relationship with this town, based mainly on her issues with the way some of the people in Gauthier had looked down on her mother. Although it wasn't as taboo anymore, in a small town like Gauthier back in the late 1970s, teenage pregnancy was still a shunable offense, especially when you pinned the pregnancy on someone many would feel was above your station.

Once Paxton was old enough, Belinda told her about the gossip that had floated around town when she'd become pregnant, but she was never ashamed of her daughter, and she never held a grudge against the town over the way they'd treated her. Paxton had not been so generous or forgiving. Bitterness still lingered when she thought of her mother being ostracized simply because she'd made the mistake of falling for the wrong boy.

Tonight, however, went a long way in soothing the resentment Paxton still clung to. There were some in Gauthier who likely whispered behind both her and Belinda's backs, but for the most part, these were good people. They stood up for their own and were always eager to show their support.

As she cleared empty glasses and plates from the tables, Paxton thanked those who had come to tonight's grand opening.

Everyone in the room stood and voices quieted as an ROTC from one of the local colleges performed the "Star-Spangled Banner" on the eight large-screen televisions that were, of course, all tuned into the much-anticipated *Monday Night Football* game between the New Orleans Saints and the Atlanta Falcons. They remained standing through the coin-toss and the kickoff.

On the very first play of the game, one of the Saints' defensive players intercepted the Falcons' quarterback's pass. The room went wild, and Paxton said a quick prayer that the place didn't fall off its pilings as it shook with the cheers and foot stomping.

She looked toward the bar and caught Belinda's smile. It was so wide Paxton knew her cheeks were probably hurting.

From the moment she had signed the bill of sale and handed over the deed, Paxton had anticipated seeing the look she saw right now on her mother's face. It made every cent worth it. Although no amount of money could ever repay her mother for the sacrifices she'd made.

Belinda would argue that Paxton had made her share of sacrifices as well, with all the nights and weekends she'd given up to work next to her in this bar, but Paxton had never looked at it that way. They were a team. They always had been.

And, finally, the teamwork was paying off.

Paxton returned to her place behind the bar. It had been well over a year since she'd poured drinks, but it had come back to her with amazing ease. She topped off several shot glasses, mixed up a frozen strawberry daiquiri in the high-powered blender she'd purchased and served up two more pitchers of beer.

As she wiped condensation from the bar, she looked

up and noticed Sawyer walking toward her. Her heart-beat tripled as she followed his easy stride toward the bar. His dark blue jeans gripped his solid, sure thighs, and the black polo shirt molded to his taut chest. Good-ness, but he looked delicious.

"What are you doing here?" Paxton asked when he approached, slinging the dish towel over her shoulder.

A slow grin spread across his face as he slid onto a bar stool. "You ask that to everybody in here tonight?"

"No, smart-ass," she said. "But this is a bit of a drive for you."

"It was worth the drive to show my support for to-night's grand opening. I know how hard you and your mom worked to make this happen."

There went that flutter again. The warm, cozy sensa-tion spread throughout her chest. "Thank you," she said. "I really appreciate the support."

"My pleasure." Paxton could feel the heat climbing up her cheeks as his eyes traced over her face. Was she actually blushing?

Sawyer looked over his shoulder. "Nice crowd in here tonight."

"I know," Paxton said, unable to contain her excite-ment. "I was hoping for a decent turnout, but this is so far beyond my expectations. I can't tell you how thrilled I am."

"You don't have to. Your eyes are sparkling. So are your mom's," Sawyer said, nodding toward Belinda, who was talking to Janice and Melvin Hodges. Pax-ton had always thought the couple was too religious to ever step foot in a bar, but apparently they had decided to face damnation so they could support her mother's new business.

"She is having the time of her life," Paxton said.

"How about you?" Sawyer asked. "Was it worth all the money and effort?"

She returned her attention to him with a triumphant smile. "Every single penny."

His eyes dropped to her lips, and the air between them was suddenly saturated with a heavy dose of desire.

"That smile looks so good on you," he said in a mesmerizingly seductive voice.

"I—thank you," Paxton replied.

Thank you? Was that the best she could come up with?

His eyes glittered with amusement as a slight smile tilted up the corner of his mouth. He shook his head. "You're stubborn as hell, but you won't be able to fight this much longer."

No further explanation was needed to spell out what he meant by this. They both knew what he was talking about, but he was right; she *was* stubborn as hell, and she was not going down without a fight.

"That's where you're wrong," she said as she wiped down the bar with the towel she'd slung over her shoulder.

Sawyer leaned forward, rising up from his bar stool. "But why fight it?" he asked. "Just think about it. If you're going back to Little Rock at the end of this project, what's the harm in us being together while you're here?"

She was ashamed to admit how tempted she was at the thought of doing just that.

"Think about it," he prodded. "We have three weeks left. There's a lot we can do in that time."

"Stop tempting me," she said.

One deliciously sexy brow arched. "So you *are*

tempted?" He leaned in even closer, putting his mouth against her ear. "Now that you've admitted it, you do know I'm just going to try harder to convince you, don't you, Paxton?"

A shudder coursed through her body at his sexy promise. God, but she wanted him.

So why not take what he was offering?

Things were completely different from three years ago. The guilt that had plagued her over taking advantage of him while he was vulnerable and suffering was a nonfactor this time.

"Pax, any idea where the margarita salt is?"

She jerked away from Sawyer and turned to her mother.

And was caught totally off guard by the look on her mother's face. Her previously smiling eyes were full of caution and mistrust.

What in the world is going on here?

"The salt?" her mother asked again, her dubious gaze still centered on Sawyer.

"It's in the storage room," Paxton said. "I put it on the top shelf."

She turned back to Sawyer and hooked a thumb toward where her mother had just stood. "You have any idea what that was about?"

Sawyer shrugged. "Maybe she wasn't expecting to see me here, either. You know, like mother, like daughter."

That could have possibly been it, but Paxton wasn't so sure. She couldn't deny that he stuck out like a bruised and battered thumb. Many of the people here worked for Sawyer's family at the lumber mill. Now that his father was no longer around, that meant they worked for Sawyer.

Interestingly enough, Paxton didn't detect even a hint of the veiled animosity that often hovered between bosses and employees. Several people approached the bar to thank Sawyer for some incentive program instituted at the mill. Others just wanted to shake his hand. The interactions were a testament to the respect the workers held for the Robertson family, and vice versa.

Paxton got that funny feeling in her stomach again, the one that suggested that maybe she'd judged Sawyer unjustly. She was certain that if she thought long and hard enough, she would be able to recall an incident back during their days at Gauthier High when Sawyer had earned the spoiled, arrogant rich-boy label she'd placed on him. But for the life of her she could not remember a single one.

Had she been wrong this entire time?

Could that mean she was also wrong about other things, like not believing Shayla when she said Sawyer had always been interested in her?

Her stomach twisted with the plethora of doubt and hopefulness swirling through it.

The Saints game ended in a heartbreaker, with the Atlanta Falcons returning the favor of that earlier interception and running it back for a touchdown. Their touchdown, however, came in the last two minutes of the game and handed them the victory.

Despite the loss, the crowd remained upbeat, and just about everyone came up to Paxton and Belinda to tell them how much they enjoyed themselves, and how they planned to be back on Saturday for the LSU football game. Her regulars all promised to be back tomorrow.

Now that Harlon's—Paxton had just accepted it would never shake that name—served real food, she suspected it would acquire a larger set of regulars.

"It's pretty late," Sawyer said when she returned to the bar. "How much longer are you staying?"

"We have to clean up."

"Do you need any help?"

Paxton couldn't keep the incredulousness off her face if she tried. She didn't try.

"What?" Sawyer asked. "I have washed dishes before, you know." He pulled the towel from her shoulder and snapped it on the bar top. "I can bust suds with the best of them."

Her sharp laugh was so loud she drew the attention of several of the people still lingering around the bar.

"You don't believe me—do you?" Sawyer asked.

"I'm trying to picture it." She looked him up and down. "No, I really don't see you rolling up your sleeves and—how did you put it? Busting suds?"

"You've pegged me all wrong," he said. He leaned in closer and whispered against her ear again, "I'm going to have fun changing the way you see me."

Decadent shivers of need cascaded along her skin as her body screamed, *Let him!*

"Now, do you need help or don't you?" Sawyer asked.

"No, she doesn't." Donovan appeared from seemingly out of nowhere, sidling up next to her and clamping his arm around her shoulder. His six-foot-two frame towered over her, much like Sawyer's. He puffed his chest out. "I'm here to help her. It's my job."

Paxton rolled her eyes as she disengaged from his hold.

Sawyer hooked a thumb at Donovan. "Is this Harlon's

grandson that you used to babysit back in high school? The one who bit Mr. Washington the year he posed as Santa Claus?"

"Yes, it is," Paxton said with a laugh. "I can't believe you remember that."

Donovan was not so amused. He gave Sawyer an assessing look from head to toe, a slow and pissed-off perusal. Paxton couldn't help but chuckle. This poor kid really thought he had a chance with her. She didn't know whether to be charmed or exasperated by him on any given day.

"I appreciate both offers to help, but I think we've got things under control. I'll see you at the office tomorrow," she told Sawyer. She looked over at Donovan. "You did a good job tonight, but you should go home and check on your grandpa."

"He's okay," Donovan said.

"Well, then, just go home and get some rest."

"You're going to miss me when I'm gone," he said. And, of course, he winked.

If she could get away with it, she would superglue his eyes shut.

"Are you really putting me out, too?" Sawyer asked.

"Yes," she said, taking him by the hand and tugging him toward the exit. She walked him to his car, which was one of the last remaining in the parking lot. It was a good thing he was driving his dad's Buick. His luxury car would have stood out among the dusty pickup trucks and dented sedans.

"So, have you thought about what I suggested?" Sawyer asked.

She cocked her head to the side. "Refresh my memory again?"

"Me, you and three weeks of no-strings-attached fun before you go back to Little Rock."

"Oh, that." She rolled her eyes. "I'm too tired to think up a good excuse to say no. Ask me again tomorrow, when I'm well rested and on my game."

He ran his hand along her hair. "There's only one answer I'll accept, and no isn't it."

"Good night, Sawyer. Thank you again for coming out here tonight."

"Maybe I'll become a regular," he said. "Especially now that I know I have competition."

She chuckled. "If you're talking about Donovan, you have nothing to worry about."

"Maybe I'll become a regular, anyway," he said. "Just because the more you see me, the harder it will be for you to turn me down." He leaned in closer to her, his lips nearly touching hers. "I'm going to make you see the real me, Pax. That's a promise."

She suffered through a full-body shudder.

Could she want him any more than she did right now? Impossible.

He got into the Buick and slowly backed away; the loose gravel kicked up from underneath the tires.

Paxton stood there for several minutes, giving herself time to come down from the stimulating high she'd been on since Sawyer had walked through the door. She returned to the kitchen to help Belinda and Jessie clean. Even though they were all exhausted, they were done in less than an hour.

As she and her mother crossed the pasture, heading for their trailer—Heinz trotting alongside them—they chatted about the success of opening night. Paxton's chest was so filled with pride she feared it would burst wide-open. Belinda's excitement was palpable. Paxton couldn't remember the last time she'd seen her so animated. So happy.

However, once they arrived home her mother's mood changed.

Paxton was adding leftover food scraps into Heinz's food bowl when Belinda came upon her, her expression devoid of the sunniness that had been there all night.

"Is there something I should know about you and Sawyer Robertson?" her mother asked.

Paxton's head popped up. "We're working together. You know that already."

"What I saw tonight looked like a bit more than just colleagues shooting the breeze."

"Really?" Paxton chuckled as she walked over to the kitchen faucet and filled a plastic cup with water.

"The question," Paxton said as she poured the water into Heinz's water bowl, "is what's going on between *you* and Sawyer. There was a weird vibe between the two of you tonight."

"I was just shocked to see someone like him in my bar."

"Someone like him? Sawyer isn't an alien," Paxton said.

"He's a rich boy from the other side of the creek."

"Just because he comes from money doesn't automatically make him a bad person," Paxton said.

Wait. Had she really just said that? Did she believe that?

Yes. She did.

"I just want you to be careful," Belinda said. "I know what it's like to have a rich boy charm the pants right off of you."

Paxton knew she was talking about her father, though she rarely thought of him in those terms. Damien Gaines was the boy who had gotten her mother pregnant. Period.

He'd come from a family of means. They weren't on the scale of the Robertsons—few in Gauthier were—but the Gaines were well-off by most standards. Back when Paxton was in high school, Belinda had imparted what Paxton considered a cautionary tale. She told her how Damien had sweet-talked her into sleeping with him, and once he found out she was pregnant he had denied it ever happened. Her mother was also adamant that she had not been with anyone else, so even though there had never been a paternity test, Paxton had no doubt that he was her father.

Not as if it mattered.

Belinda had been both mother and father to her, and she'd done a damn fine job of it.

Damien Gaines now lived over in Saint Pierre, a small town just east of Gauthier. Paxton would run into him from time to time, but she never so much as nodded his way. He was a nonfactor.

Her mother had always been afraid of Paxton falling into the teen pregnancy trap, even though she hadn't been a teen in nearly two decades.

"Mom, you don't have to worry about me," Paxton assured her. "I know how to take care of myself. You taught me well."

"I know you can take care of yourself physically. I'm worried about your heart."

Paxton gathered her in a hug and squeezed. "I can take care of that, too."

And she would. When it came to her heart, she would do everything she could to protect it.

* * *

Using the flashlight app on his phone to illuminate the dead bolt, Sawyer inserted one of two keys that he suspected opened the lock on the front door of the building he hadn't stepped foot in since his dad purchased it more than four years ago. The telling click of the lock rang out into the still night; the only accompanying sound was the howl of an owl off in the distance.

Once inside, Sawyer used the phone to locate the building's lights, flipping them on and breathing a sigh of relief.

"Good job, Mike," he said.

Michael Bastian, who had worked for years as a foreman at the lumber mill, had taken over maintenance of the building soon after his father had bought it. It was just before the cancer diagnosis, when Sawyer's life had taken yet another heart-wrenching turn.

He spotted a push broom leaning against the wall. He grabbed the thick handle and, despite the room being virtually spotless, proceeded to shove the thick bristles along the vinyl tile flooring. The monotonous motion was surprisingly soothing, giving his brain a much-needed break from all the thoughts that had been swirling around in there for the past couple of days.

Between the plans for this flood protection system that were starting to make him more and more nervous by the second and what seemed like an insurmountable task of breaking past that barrier Paxton had built up against him, Sawyer didn't have time to think of much else. But a germ of an idea had managed to burrow its way into his head after talking with so many of the mill's workers at Belinda Jones's sports bar.

It wasn't until he'd passed it on his way to the bar's grand opening that Sawyer even remembered exactly where this building was located. He didn't get out to Landreaux all that often. He didn't have a reason to. Other than one small filling station that doubled as a grocery store, a few churches and the bar, the area was made up of mainly residences.

But many of those residents were his father's loyal workers, men and women who made it to work at the lumber mill before the sun came up. Hardworking people whose families would benefit from a place where they could hang out in the afternoon and on weekends, a place like this building.

Over the past four years Sawyer would get the occasional phone call from Mike, inquiring about plans for the space, but up until now Sawyer didn't have an answer. During the final year of his life, he and his dad never had a chance to discuss it. Sawyer had been content to let the building sit there unused.

Until now.

A flash of light through the uncovered window caught his attention.

There wasn't another house for a half mile on either side of the stretch of highway that led to the bridge over Landreaux Creek. Sawyer carried the push broom with him as he made his way to the door.

A rusty Ford pickup, circa 1981, pulled up alongside the Buick. The driver's side door opened and the overhead light illuminated the truck's cab, revealing Mike Bastian's leathery face.

Sawyer broke out in a smile as he leaned the broom handle against the outside wall and walked over to the truck.

"How're you doing, old man?" he asked, clamping Mike's callous palm in a handshake before bringing him in for a hug.

Mike returned the hug, then slapped Sawyer on the shoulder.

"Don't you go scaring me like this. You had me thinking somebody had broken in here. Myra Jacobs called Felicity at the house and told her she'd spotted the lights on here but didn't see my truck. You'd better be happy I didn't grab my shotgun. Your behind could be full of buckshot right now."

"It's nice to know so many people are keeping an eye out," Sawyer said, patting Mike on the back as they returned to the building.

Mike took him on a quick tour, showing him where he'd repaired the wall after frozen pipes during last winter's brief freeze had burst. Mike had also taken liberties with the kitchenette, installing a new wash bin he'd found for a cheap price on Craigslist.

"Why didn't you tell me about this?" Sawyer said, reaching in his back pocket for his wallet. "How much do I owe you for it?"

Mike waved him off. "I'm not worrying about no money, boy. If I didn't spend it on the sink, Felicity would spend it on all those knickknacks crowding the house. Teapots are her new thing. Got more damn teapots in that house than the British."

Laughing as he stuffed the wallet back into his pocket, Sawyer followed Mike into the main area of the building.

"So, what you doing all the way out here?" he asked. Sawyer told him about the bar's grand opening, which, of course, Mike had already heard about.

"I decided to drop in here and see how the building was holding up, since it was on the way home," Sawyer told him. "You've taken good care of it."

"Nothing else to do now that I'm retired from the mill," Mike said with a shrug.

"Don't you think it's time we do something with this place?" Sawyer asked. "My dad wouldn't want it to just sit here, giving you an excuse to get away from Felicity every now and then."

"You'd better not tell her that," Mike warned.

"I won't." He laughed; then he sobered. "I'm serious, Mike. My dad and I never discussed it, but I think we could maybe turn this place into a rec center for the families of the mill workers who live over here in Landreaux. There are a lot of them on this side of the creek. Don't you think they would appreciate a place for their families, something close to home that doesn't require them driving all the way to downtown Gauthier?"

He walked to the far end of the room. "I'm picturing five or so computer stations here. And maybe in the corner over there we could do a reading area. Hell, this place is big enough to put in a wall or two. They can hold several different events at one time."

Sawyer couldn't be sure he'd ever seen Mike wearing a smile as big as the one on his face right now. On the average person, it would barely be considered a grin.

"Earl did a pretty good job with you," Mike said, that smile widening even more. "When your mama passed on he was scared as hell that he would mess you up, but Cheryl Ann would be proud of the son he raised."

Sawyer couldn't deny the pride warming his chest. "Thanks, Mike. That means a lot coming from you." His hands on his hips, Sawyer looked around the vast empty space. "So, what do you think?"

Mike patted him on the back. "I think I got myself a new excuse to get away from Felicity's teapots."

Chapter 6

Paxton pulled into the gravel parking lot of the Gauthier Lions Club's lodge, surprised to find it empty. Was she the first one here?

"Hmm, I guess miracles really do happen," she murmured as she checked her lipstick in the rearview mirror.

A moment later, Sawyer's gleaming BMW pulled up next to her car. He looked over at her and smiled. He wore dark sunglasses, and, my goodness, but they looked good against his rich mahogany skin. Paxton sucked in a swift breath, praying it would help to regulate her heart rate.

"Lord, I want this man," she breathed. Getting out of her car, she sucked in another calming breath. Her blood was still simmering after last night's near kiss. She needed to find some control if she was going to make it through today without taking Sawyer up on his offer.

And she was determined not to take him up on his offer.

Maybe.

Sawyer met her at his front fender, sans sunglasses.

"Good morning," he greeted her.

Two seconds had passed and she'd managed to refrain from pushing him onto the hood of his car and climbing on top of him. That was a good start.

"Good morning," Paxton returned. She nodded toward his car. "I see you got your baby back."

"And not a moment too soon. I couldn't take another day in the Buick. I was just about to start jogging to work."

Her gaze immediately dropped to his well-toned chest, which no doubt benefited from the evening jogs he told her he took after work. Her eyes darted back up to his, which creased slightly at the edges with his smile.

"You can look," he said with a grin. "I don't mind."

Paxton rolled her eyes and released a frustrated sigh.

"Hey, you two! Good morning!"

Paxton turned to find Mya Anderson striding toward them.

"Thanks for coming out so early," Paxton said to her in greeting. "I appreciate you taking the time out to show us the storm damage."

Mya Dubois had created a gossip firestorm when she left Gauthier weeks after high school graduation, and she was the subject of even more gossip when she returned fifteen years later to attend her grandfather's funeral. Instead of hightailing it back to New York, she'd remained in Gauthier and eventually married her old high school sweetheart, Corey Anderson.

Corey and Mya had discovered Gauthier's recent claim to fame, the room in the Gauthier Law Firm that had been confirmed as a stop on the Underground Railroad. Mya, who had once shunned her hometown, had become Gauthier's biggest advocate. She now served as a pseudomayor/community leader, following in her grandmother Eloise Dubois's footsteps.

"I should be thanking the two of you," Mya said. "Getting that millage tax passed was one hurdle, but making sure the best flood protection system possible is put into place is what really matters. Having two life-long residents handling this project is more than I could have ever hoped for."

"It's going to be more than sufficient," Paxton said. She glanced quickly at Sawyer, who's expression remained neutral. "From what I hear, your grandmother and the rest of the members of the Gauthier Civic Association had a lot to do with getting out the vote and pushing the measure."

"To be honest, they didn't have to do much pushing after Tropical Storm Lucy blew through. The flooding was unprecedented, and in so many areas that hardly see standing water in the streets, let alone the kind of flooding we all saw with that storm. It became obvious pretty quickly just how much this new flood protection system is needed." Mya motioned for them to follow her. "Let me show you some of the damage that occurred here."

They entered the lodge, which was known mostly for the monthly pancake breakfast it hosted but which also served as an after-school day care center.

"Insurance covered a fair amount of the damage, but not all of it. The Lions Club held fund-raisers to cover the rest of the repairs. The building was out of commission for months."

"Isn't this where they hold the youth summer camp?" Sawyer asked.

"Usually, but they couldn't hold it here last summer. The school board allowed the organizers to hold an abbreviated two-week summer program in the school cafeteria, but the school also took in some water and had to undergo its own repairs."

Paxton studied the drawings taped to the walls, crayon masterpieces with smiling stick figures. There were also posters with positive affirmations, healthy living guides and quotes encouraging kids to eat right and engage in at least sixty minutes of physical activity per day.

"They were still building this place when I left for Little Rock," she murmured. "It looks as if they do a lot here with the kids."

"It has been a great addition to the community," Mya said. "The previous building was much smaller."

"It's still a pretty long drive for some in the community," Sawyer commented. "There isn't a place like this in the Landreaux area, is there?"

"No," Paxton confirmed with a shake of her head. "I wish there were. We could use something like this on the other side of the creek. There's so little for kids to do there."

He stared at her for a moment, a curious look about him, before redirecting his attention back to Mya. "Do you know how high the water got in here?"

"Actually, I can show you." Mya motioned for them to follow her. "They still haven't changed out the drywall in the storage closet."

She flipped on a light in a closet at the rear of the room. It was faint, but Paxton could make out the line that rimmed the wall. It was nearly a foot from the floor.

"Goodness, there was that much water?" she asked. "How long did it take to recede?"

"That was another thing. Because the ground was already so saturated and the rivers nearing flood stages because of a heavy rain the week before, the water took days to recede. Everyone I talked to said that they had never seen anything like this, especially in this part of town."

Paxton nodded. "My mom said the same. Thankfully, Harlon's Bar is raised. It would have gotten a lot more damage if it were sitting on a slab instead of pilings."

Just the thought sent a spiral of unease skittering down Paxton's spine. She'd heard the stories and seen pictures and videos, but it wasn't until this very moment, until she saw with her own eyes how high the water had climbed, that it truly sank in for her. If it had rose a foot, what would stop it from rising two feet, or three feet, with the next big rain event?

What if that perfect storm scenario Sawyer had talked about came to pass?

Actually seeing the damage made the importance of what they were doing hit home for Paxton like nothing else ever could. Her mind immediately conjured up the topography maps stretched across the conference room table. How much had the landscape changed since they were drawn up? If she looked at them right now, would it show that this area of Gauthier was elevated and thus shouldn't have flooded?

She had faith in her team at Bolt-Myer, and didn't

want to question the work they'd put into this project, but the writing was literally on the wall. That faint waterline signified so much.

Sawyer was right. There was something going on here, and Paxton had the sinking feeling that if they didn't get to the root cause before they started working on the design phase of the project, Gauthier was destined to see a repeat of what had happened with Tropical Storm Lucy.

Their next stop was the elementary school. The damage sustained had not been as extensive as at the Lion's Club, but several classrooms were *still* out of commission nearly a year after the flooding.

"There were several homes that were damaged, too, right?" Sawyer asked as they walked along the gravel lot behind the school.

"A few, but many of those have been repaired," Mya said.

"We should still talk to the owners," Paxton said. "I want to get an idea of how bad the flooding was and how close it has come to anything else they've seen in recent years."

"We should probably tour the animal shelter, too," Mya said.

Paxton stopped short, her stomach dropping. "The animal shelter?" she asked. "I didn't realize it had been hit, too. Shayla never told me."

Mya nodded. "It was. Thankfully, all the animals were saved. Callie Webber, the vet over in Maplesville, volunteered her practice as a makeshift shelter. But it was all still pretty traumatic for the animals."

Panic filled Paxton's senses. That animal shelter had been one of the biggest sources of comfort to her as a teenager. Just the thought of the animals being in harm's way stole the breath from her lungs.

She turned to Sawyer. "We have to go," she said. "I have to see it for myself."

Even though Sawyer braced himself for the rush of memories he knew would hit the moment he stepped through the doors of the animal shelter, he was still taken aback. It looked the same. It smelled the same. This place where he'd spent so much of his young life lusting over Paxton.

When she wasn't helping her mother at Harlon's, Paxton was at this shelter, tending to mange-ridden dogs and flea-infested cats. She spent so many hours there after school and on the weekend, so, of course, Sawyer had used every excuse he could think of to be there, too.

He'd considered signing up as a volunteer but thought it would be too obvious, so he'd gotten creative. He'd lied about collecting pet food donations and instead had used money from his allowance to buy it, simply to have an excuse to come to the shelter. He would ride around Gauthier looking for stray animals to rescue. Any excuse he could find.

He still remembered the day he heard Malachi Walker complaining in the weight room about having to deal with the stink of the animal shelter because it's where Shayla Kirkland, his assigned tutor, had to tutor him. It was like finding a golden ticket. Despite being a straight A student, Sawyer purposely failed two math tests so that coach would sign him up for tutoring.

Three days a week for two months straight, Sawyer would come over to the animal shelter. While Shayla tutored him in mathematical equations that he could complete in his sleep, he'd watch Paxton out of the corner of his eye as she showered the affection he'd wanted from her onto helpless strays. The girl who was always so tough with people had a soft spot when it came to animals.

Sawyer cringed when he thought back to his awkward attempts to get her to talk to him. He'd tried to ask about the different breeds, or engage her in conversation about types of vaccinations, but other than a quick hello, Paxton barely said a word to him.

After the first couple of weeks he'd told himself to forget about her. He didn't even have to snap his fingers to get a girl to notice him. He was the star quarterback of the football team. He always had enough dollars in his pocket for dinner and a movie on Saturday night. And even Sawyer could admit that when he looked in the mirror the guy staring back at him was pretty easy on the eyes. He had been a damn good catch back in high school.

But none of those things—the looks, the money, the popularity—none of it had made a difference to Paxton. It wasn't as if she played hard to get, either. It was like he'd been invisible to her, like he wasn't even on her radar.

She may have felt that way about him in high school, but Sawyer knew for a fact that she damn well saw him now. She could no longer ignore him.

Actually, she could. Because, at the moment, all of her attention was focused on the animals. As soon as they entered the shelter she went straight for a pen that held a litter of puppies. Everything about her seemed to change in an instant. She went from being the hard-core professional back to the girl who used to spend hours here every week taking care of sick and frightened animals.

Sawyer studied the soft look on her face as she got down on the floor in her skirt and cuddled with the puppies, taking turns holding each close to her chest.

He propped his shoulder against the wall and casually slid his hands into his pockets. Tilting his head to the side, he asked, "Where did the love of dogs come from?"

Paxton didn't so much as glance up at him. She had eyes only for the puppies.

"I just always loved dogs," she said with a shrug. "It used to drive Belinda crazy every time I would find a stray and bring it home. She used to say she had a hard enough time keeping me fed—she couldn't keep every stray in Landreaux's belly full, too. She's the one who told me to work at the shelter."

Paxton shook her head as she lovingly petted the mutt's thick fur. "There's something about strays that calls to me," she said. "They're tough, resilient. They have to be in order to survive." She looked up at him. "I guess they remind me of me and my mom."

Sawyer didn't know what to say to that. He just continued to stare at her, pondering her statement.

A couple of minutes later, the shelter's director, Webster Detellier, came over to speak with them. His mother, Gina, ran the shelter back when they were in high school, and Webster would often be there with them after school. Sawyer's jealousy over how well Paxton and Webster got along used to eat him up inside.

It wasn't until years later that Sawyer discovered his jealousy was unwarranted. He often ran into Webster and his partner, Glenn, every now and then on his evening jogs. They lived a couple of blocks down the street from him.

Still, Sawyer couldn't deny that seeing her in this setting again had drummed up a cadre of feelings that he hadn't felt in a while. Longing. Inadequacy. That ridiculous adolescent hopefulness that he would figure out a way to win the girl. Sucking in a deep breath to steady himself against the onslaught of emotions rioting through him, Sawyer approached them.

He greeted Webster, then asked, "Do you know if the shelter had ever had this type of flooding in the past?"

"Sandalwood Drive slopes down toward the creek, so it may get standing water from time to time, but nothing like we got with Lucy," Webster said. "Oh, by the way, thanks for the donation," he told Sawyer.

"You're welcome," Sawyer said.

Paxton's confused expression begged for an explanation. Before he could say anything, Webster did it for him.

"His family's foundation made a huge donation to the shelter last year. It helped to vaccinate every animal. We're still purchasing food with the money from the donation."

Sawyer shrugged. "It's the foundation that was started in my mother's name. She had a soft spot for animals, but my dad was allergic so we couldn't have any. I know my mom would approve of helping the shelter."

"That's wonderful," Paxton said, her eyes soft and full of admiration.

As ridiculous as it seemed, her admiration annoyed him. Why did it take something like that for her to see him as someone worthy of her respect? Unlike his shenanigans with the pet food back when they were in high school, there were no ulterior motives to his actions these days. He gave out of a sense of responsibility, out of respect for his parents, who, despite their money, had raised him with a sense of humility few with their means would even think to do.

It had always irritated him that Paxton couldn't be bothered to see past his moneyed upbringing. If she had only taken the time to look, she would have realized that he had *never* lived a life of privilege. Sure, his father had built a company that grossed millions, but Earl Robertson had come from humble beginnings, something he'd never forgotten. He never allowed Sawyer to take anything for granted. And Sawyer was grateful for every lesson he'd been taught.

That was why he did everything he could to live up to his parents' expectations, even at the expense of his own happiness.

Even to this day it made his stomach hurt to think about everything he'd sacrificed in order to fulfill his father's final wish, marrying a girl he didn't love. His marriage had been a mistake from the very beginning. He'd known it. Angelique, his ex-wife, had known it, as well. They'd both gone along with it in order to make their families happy, but they both knew the marriage was never going to last.

Sawyer shook that thought out of his head.

That murky water needed to remain where it had been since his divorce: under the bridge. He needed to focus on the things that really mattered. Mainly, figuring out a way to make the girl he'd always wanted see him as someone she could potentially share her life with.

It wasn't a pipe dream to contemplate it. They had chemistry. He refused to believe what had happened be-

tween them three years ago was a onetime thing. He'd
felt something that night, and he knew Paxton had felt
it, too. He needed her to actually *believe* in it.

She giggled—actually *giggled*—when three of the
puppies ganged up on her, climbing up her chest at the
same time. Seeing her so carefree right now, it made him
aware of just how few times he'd seen her this way. She'd
always had a seriousness about her, even back when they
were in high school.

Sawyer could recall with startling clarity the day he'd
fallen for her. It was during their sophomore year, when
Paxton had discovered that a group of their classmates
were planning a cruel practical joke on Mrs. Baker, their
substitute science teacher. She had always quietly flown
under the radar, never doing anything to stand out from
the crowd.

Until that day.

She called out their classmates before they were able
to play the joke. She had been brave enough to do something that Sawyer hadn't had the courage to do for fear of
losing cool points in front of his friends. She'd changed
his way of thinking that day. Because of her bravery,
Sawyer decided that his convictions, and not his social
standing, would dictate how he conducted himself.

That day in science class, he saw Paxton Jones as
more than just the girl who hung out with Shayla. He'd
finally taken notice of how beautiful she was underneath her unassuming clothes and reserved demeanor.
She didn't clamor for attention. She didn't have to—at
least as far as Sawyer was concerned.

From that day forward he'd set out to win her approval.

But he wanted more than just her approval. He wanted

her to see him as more than just a jock or a spoiled rich boy. He wanted her to see him as someone who was worthy of her.

He wanted *her*. Damn, did he want her.

As he watched her with the animals, showering them all with love, allowing them to climb all over her as she sat on the floor in her pricey business skirt, Sawyer was pummeled with all the reasons he continued to want her. Underneath that no-nonsense facade, she had a softer side that he'd fallen in love with so long ago.

He had to make this woman his. *Had* to. He'd waited too long for her, and he'd be damned if he let her get away this time.

They still had a couple of other sites to visit before they returned to the office, but Sawyer couldn't bring himself to break up her puppy love fest. He selfishly wanted to see this side of her for as long as he possibly could.

After another half hour had passed, Paxton was finally able to tear herself away from the animals. She thanked Webster for his continued work with the shelter and, looking over her shoulder with every step she took, reluctantly walked out of the building.

Sawyer could tell she was still shaken up. Knowing that the animals she'd cared about so much had been in danger seemed to be a shock to her system, but her demeanor changed back to the efficient and practical Paxton before he could offer her the comfort he desperately wanted to give.

"See you back at the office?" she asked, her eyes darting over his shoulder to the shelter again.

"Sure," Sawyer said. He looked back at the shelter, then to her. "Are you okay, Pax?"

She shook her head and gave him a false smile. "Of course. I'll call the Jazzy Bean and order some lunch on the way."

"That sounds good," Sawyer said.

She nodded; then, with one last look at the shelter, she got in her car and drove away.

Chapter 7

"Hey, you okay over there?"

Despite his subdued tone, Paxton jumped at the sound of Sawyer's voice coming from just over her shoulder. She didn't turn, but continued to stare out the window, watching the breeze blow gently through the arching branches of the oak trees that peppered Heritage Park.

"I'm okay," she said. "Just…thinking." She took several steps back, realizing that she was crowding his work space. "Sorry for being in the way."

"No," he said. "You can stay where you are. I'll be at the conference table for the rest of the afternoon, anyway. I just needed these."

Paxton glanced over her shoulder to see him picking up the master materials list from his desk. A list that was based on maps that were likely unreliable and could lead to tragedy for her small hometown.

She shut her eyes tight and fought back the truth she could no longer deny. Turning to Sawyer, she folded her arms across her chest and ran her hands along them.

The smooth dark brown skin on his forehead creased as he frowned at her. "Are you sure you're okay, Pax?"

She shook her head. "Not really. It's hard to be okay after what we saw today."

Sawyer set the binder back on his desk and took a couple of steps toward her. The concern in his gaze warmed her from the inside out, or maybe it was just her body's reaction to the way his powerful, sinewy body moved, both purposeful and graceful.

To say he was handsome seemed woefully inadequate. His compelling brown eyes, generous mouth and sharp chin belonged in a magazine spread.

"It was a pretty heavy day," Sawyer said.

"Sobering," Paxton said. She pulled her bottom lip between her teeth and soaked in the calming scene on the other side of the window before looking back at him. "Both Belinda and Shayla tried to describe how bad the flooding had been, but it took seeing it with my own eyes to truly understand."

"Same here," Sawyer said. He crossed his arms over his chest and leaned against the wall. "It's scary to think of how much worse it could have been."

Studying his strained expression, Paxton found the same worry that had been eating away at her since they left the animal shelter.

"What if that worst-case scenario happens, Sawyer? And what if it isn't just a tropical storm the next time? This town could be devastated."

"The possibility is there. If Gauthier is hit by a category three hurricane—hell, even a strong, slow-moving category two—the damage would be significant."

"Some people in those low-lying areas could lose everything," Paxton whispered. "The animal shelter…" She trailed off, unable to finish the thought.

She turned fully toward him.

"You're right about the maps," Paxton said. It was time she owned up to her mistake. "You tried to tell me, but I'm stubborn. And I don't like anyone proving me wrong. But I'm also a realist, and it cannot be ignored. Not after what I saw today."

Sawyer's eyes shut. He blew out a relieved sigh, his shoulders going limp.

"Thank you," he said.

"I'm planning to contact my supervisor at Bolt-Myer this afternoon. I'll tell him your theory, along with the evidence we saw today. It's going to set us back, both time-wise and with the budget, but we need to get those surveyors here before we move forward. We need to figure out what went wrong with Tropical Storm Lucy, because something definitely went wrong."

"I can be in on the call if you want me to explain it," he offered.

Paxton held up her hand. "I want to talk to him first. If I need you to explain the mechanics in more detail, I'll call you in." She released another sober breath and looked across the room at her desk. Her cell phone seemed so innocuous, but the call she needed to make could determine the course of her career with Bolt-Myer. She had so much riding on this project, but Gauthier's safety trumped it all.

"I should call him now," Paxton said. "The sooner we get the ball rolling, the better. I just… I need a breather."

Sawyer gestured toward the window with his chin. "It's a pretty day out there. How about a walk?"

Paxton returned her gaze to the inviting view, her spirits lifting at just the thought. She looked back at him to find him looking at her with expectation.

He'd been such a surprise today. Actually, he'd been a surprise, period. From his willingness to set aside petty arguments and work together over this past week and a half to his driving out to Landreaux to support Belinda's grand opening, to learning about his huge donation to the animal shelter.

And that he possibly used to visit it back when they were kids just to see her.

Something warm and significant began to swirl in her belly. It had taken a while to accept it, but Paxton was starting to believe that she'd read Sawyer Robertson all wrong.

She *wanted* to be wrong about him. Because if he wasn't the pampered rich playboy she'd made him out to be in her mind, and was instead the warmhearted, generous man she'd witnessed since they began this project, it could change…everything.

A smile curled up the edge of her mouth.

"An afternoon stroll around Heritage Park is exactly what I need. But only if you join me."

Sawyer's smile matched hers. "That was never a question."

Paxton left a note on Carmen's desk, letting her know where they would be in case anyone came to the law practice looking for them. Even though they had yet to be visited by anyone from the community regarding the proposed flood protection system, being available to answer questions was one of their duties during this phase of the project.

She locked up using the key Matt had given them, and she and Sawyer then walked the short distance along the brick sidewalk to Heritage Park.

They entered underneath the arching wrought iron entranceway. Fragrant vines of coral honeysuckle twined within the sign's intricate lacework. The park, like most of the downtown area, had experienced a resurgence in the past few years. Various clubs and civic organizations took turns maintaining the grounds, and every six months there was a community-wide cleanup day, where everyone pitched in to do their part in keeping downtown Gauthier beautiful.

They were even dabbling in a bit of culture. An art installation was on display in the park. Several steel pieces—nothing that Paxton could decipher the meaning of—surrounded the park's central feature, a classic wooden waterwheel that, after years of sitting idle, was finally churning again.

Instead of checking out the artwork, Paxton headed straight for her favorite area of the park, the arbor. In the spring its rustic, spindly branches were covered in sweet-scented wisteria, fostering the perfect hideaway to steal a few moments of peace.

"I love this place," Paxton said, pulling in a deep breath even though the last blooms of wisteria had left with the hot summer sun. "On my list of top ten things I've missed about Gauthier this past year, this park is number two."

"What's number one?"

"My dog, of course," Paxton said.

He chuckled. "Not your mom?"

She shook her head. "Belinda and I talked on the phone every single day, but I missed not having Heinz around to nuzzle."

"Why didn't you bring him with you to Arkansas?"

Paxton shrugged. "I have a condo in Little Rock. Heinz needs space to run. And he's always been Belinda's companion just as much as he's been mine. I didn't even bring him with me when I bought my house over on Pine Street here in Gauthier. I couldn't take him away from everything he's known."

"You sold that house, right?"

She nodded.

"Why?"

Paxton's forehead scrunched up with her confused frown. "Because I was moving."

"So Little Rock wasn't just a trial run. You plan to stay there?"

Her steps slowed until she stopped completely. With a shake of her head, Paxton admitted, "I still don't know."

Sawyer leaned back against one of the arbor's thick support beams and shoved his hands in his pockets.

"Can I ask you something?" he asked.

The weighted tone of his voice told Paxton she probably didn't want to hear what he had to say, but she decided not to be a coward for once and answered, "Go ahead."

"Did you leave because of what happened between us?"

She'd expected his question would be along these lines, but she was still a bit awed by his boldness.

"That happened three years ago, Sawyer. I left last year, two years *after* you were already married and living in Chicago," she pointed out. "Why would you think you had anything to do with me leaving?"

He hunched his shoulders, looking chagrined. "Wishful thinking."

"So you wish that I was still so affected by that one night we spent together that I had to pick up and leave everything I love?"

"When you put it *that* way it makes me seem arrogant."

Her brow arched. "You think?"

She was proud of the calm facade she was able to maintain. Because the truth was he *did* have something to do with her leaving. She'd wanted him for so long but had convinced herself that there was no way a poor girl from Landreaux could ever be with one of the richest guys in town. Then three years ago, in a night that she still dreamed about all too often, it had all changed. She'd fulfilled her longtime fantasy. And after just that one taste, she knew it would never be enough.

Paxton also knew she would never find someone living here in Gauthier who made her feel what Sawyer had made her feel that night. She'd left for Little Rock hoping to find his replacement out there somewhere.

It had been a fool's mission. There was no one else out there who could replace him.

But, then again, after what she'd learned over the past few days, it was possible that finding a replacement was unnecessary. If Shayla was to be believed, the real thing had wanted her all along.

"I have a question for you," Paxton said. Sawyer looked over at her, his brows arching. "I was talking to Shayla yesterday and she mentioned that time in high school when she tutored you in math."

"Okay," Sawyer said.

"She pointed out something that I hadn't really considered back then." She backed herself up to the support beam opposite his and leaned against it, crossing her arms over her chest. "You were one of the best students in our class. You didn't really need tutoring," she said.

He slowly shook his head. "No, I didn't."

"So, why were you getting tutored?"

His focused gaze remained on her, staring intently. "I'm going to let you figure that one out on your own," he said. "Because, if I remember correctly, you were pretty sharp yourself."

A bead of shock coursed down her spine as her mouth fell open. "Are you kidding me? You really came to the animal shelter to see me?"

"What do you think, Paxton?"

"But…why?" she asked.

"*Why?* It isn't that hard to figure out."

Her eyes widened even more. They grew so wide Paxton was afraid she wouldn't be able to close them again.

"That's just crazy," she said with an awe-filled breath.

"Why is it so hard to believe that I had a thing for you back in high school?"

"Because it is," she said. "Girls threw themselves at you left and right. Prettier girls. More popular girls. Girls who were known to put out. Why would you have wanted to date me back then?"

"Oh, I don't know," he said with a casual shrug, but his voice belied the nonchalant body language. "You were smart, cute, tough. You didn't just fall in line with what everyone else did. You actually had a mind of your own, and you weren't afraid to use it, no matter what other people thought about you."

"And you found that…attractive?"

"Extremely attractive," he said. "I still do."

She sucked in the deepest breath possible. "Don't say that, Sawyer."

"Why?" He pushed away from the beam and started toward her, his slow and steady stride like a panther's stalking its prey. He stopped mere inches from her, his hard chest incredibly close to hers.

The image of how it looked naked, shimmering with sweat, ripped with muscles, flashed before her eyes. That image was imbued on her brain, a sexy, sensual reminder of her one unforgettable night with him.

Paxton's eyes shut as a tidal wave of want crashed through her.

"Tell me, Pax," he whispered. His warm breath fluttered against her skin. "Why don't you want to hear how much I want you?"

"Because…" She managed to speak past the lust wedged in her throat.

"Is it because it makes you think about how much you want me?" He leaned in closer, his lips a hairbreadth from hers. "Tell me you want me, Paxton. Admit it."

She shook her head. In a desperate whisper, she said, "I don't want to fall for you, Sawyer."

His deep chuckle reverberated against her skin.

"Don't worry, love," he said as he closed in on her. "I'll make it worth the fall."

It started out slow, this kiss she had secretly been wanting since the last time he'd kissed her. But his pace quickened with lightning speed. Just as it had the night she'd driven him home after he drank too much at Harlon's, the night he'd stripped her clothes from her body right in the middle of his parents' living room. The night she'd gripped his naked hips in her hands, dropped to her knees and took his sinfully hard flesh into her mouth.

Now it was his tongue invading her mouth, pushing past the seam of her lips and thrusting inside. As his tongue explored, his hands slipped onto her hips and then to her sides and finally up her back. His fingertips pressed into the small of her back before inching lower, grasping her butt. He tugged her closer to him, his body hardening against her stomach.

Paxton moaned.

God, she'd wanted this. Had craved it. How foolish she'd been to try to find it with other men. No one could hold a candle to the way Sawyer commanded her body.

Her nipples grew tight and achy, the sheer and lace of her bra abrading the quickly hardening buds. She rested her arms on his broad shoulders and ran her palms along the back of his head, pulling him closer.

Emotions she had been too afraid to feel flowed through her as he moved his lips from her mouth to trail them down her jaw and along her neck. His touch was so loving, almost worshipful. It made her pulse with pleasure with every single caress. His featherlight kisses triggered goose bumps. They elevated along her skin, popping up wherever he touched.

He nudged his nose behind her ear and whispered, "It's a risk to go any further in a public park, but I'm willing to go all the way if you are."

Even as his words caused a shudder to run through her, they jerked Paxton out of her sensual daze. She couldn't get lost in his kiss again. She wouldn't. She still shouldered so much guilt from the last time they did this. She couldn't take on any more.

"I can't," she said, pulling slightly away. She gave

him a gentle push when what she really wanted to do
was pull him closer.

Dammit. She *so* didn't want to stop.

But she knew she should. After the way she'd preyed
on his vulnerabilities the last time, using him for her
own pleasure yet again would just complicate things.
They still had to work together; she could not afford
complications.

He swooped in for another kiss, but she held him
back. "Stop," she said.

Paxton could feel the reluctance in the way his shoulders dropped, but he backed away.

When he looked at her his expression was a mixture
of annoyance and lingering desire.

"Why do you keep doing that?" he asked. "For someone who's so damn smart, you keep making this same
stupid move. We can be good together, Pax. Can't you
see that?"

"No," she said, straightening her blouse, which had
been skewed during their unbelievably heated kiss.

"Why not? Why is that so hard for you to accept?"

"You want to know why?" she asked, finding her
footing again. "Because this isn't a fairy tale. This is
the real world. And in the real world Paxton Jones from
the wrong side of Landreaux Creek is not the kind of
girl people expect to see on Sawyer Robertson's arm. It
just doesn't happen."

"Who cares what people expect? And in whose world
are you talking about? Because in *my* real world, we're
damn near perfect for each other. We fit, Pax. Accept
that."

"We do not," she argued. She gestured to him. "Look
at you. You're Sawyer Robertson. Prom king. Captain of

the football team. It was like the damn sea parted every time you walked down the hallway."

"That was twenty years ago. Get over it." She jumped back at his tone. "And if you hadn't been so hell-bent on making me into whatever untouchable, unattainable thing you created in your head, you could have been walking down that hallway with me, right by my side."

Even as he said the words, Paxton still couldn't bring herself to believe them. They were in direct opposition to everything she'd believed for too many years for her to just accept it as truth.

"If anyone is to blame for us not being together in the real world, it's you," he said. "You're the one who closed yourself off. You never even gave me a chance."

She stared at him for several heartbeats, her blood moving so swiftly through her veins she could actually hear it.

"Like you said, that was twenty years ago. The distant past. It makes no sense to talk about it now, right?"

"Right," he said. "Forget high school. I want to talk about the here and now."

"Okay," she said. She crossed her arms over her chest. "Let's say we do it. Say we sleep together. Not once, not twice, but for the next few weeks. Me and you, every single night."

"I can get with that plan."

"What happens after that?" Paxton asked. "Would you really consider there being anything more between us than just sex?"

"Why wouldn't I, Paxton? Do you really believe your own bullshit about the two of us not being together because I grew up with money and you didn't?"

Her shoulders deflated as she suddenly became too

exhausted for this conversation, especially after the whirlwind emotional roller coaster she'd been on with this morning's tour.

"I don't care how you slice it, Sawyer. It's the same pie. You get the bigger piece because you come from money."

He pitched his head back and let out a curse. "This is insane."

"I agree, just not on the same thing that you do. I think it's insane for you to think that there could ever be more between us than that one night. We are too different, Sawyer. We've *always* been too different."

His jaw grew rigid as he stared at her with an intensity that made her nerves stand on end.

"Just tell me one thing," he said, his voice low and thick with accusation. "If the thought of the two of us being together is so damn improbable to you, why did you sleep with me at all?"

"Simple," Paxton said with a casual shrug, hating herself for the lie she was about to tell. "I wanted sex."

The sting of those three words hurt more than Sawyer could have imagined. The defiant lift to her chin stung even more.

But the sting only lasted for a second. Because Sawyer wasn't buying it.

She'd tried this before, when she told him she was over that night they'd shared together, and he'd proven her wrong. He would prove her wrong again, because it had *not* been about just sex that night.

She could tell herself that lie all she wanted to. She may even believe it. But he would be damned if he let her go on believing it for one more day. She was going to admit that she felt something for him.

"So, that's all I was for you that night?" he asked in a deceptively casual voice. "Just an available body?"

His gaze skimmed her features, relishing the discomfort he caught when her eyes flashed to his.

Good. She deserved to feel uncomfortable.

Instead of answering his questions, she crossed her arms over her chest again and asked her own. "Are you saying it was more than just a drunken night of sex for you?"

"Only one of us was drunk that night," Sawyer said. And it had been him. He knew she wasn't drunk because when he'd first offered to buy her a drink she'd declined, telling him that she never drank when she tended bar. She eventually relented after he'd pleaded with her, indulging in only one shot of tequila.

"And I wasn't all that drunk," Sawyer continued. "I had a few, but it's not as if I got trashed that night. I was alert enough to do—" he made a slow and deliberate perusal of her body "—things," he finished.

He caught the way her chest rose and fell with her swift intake of breath, and he knew she was thinking of all the things he'd done to her that night. Things he'd wanted to continue doing to her, over and over, well into the morning.

If she had bothered to stay in his bed.

But she hadn't. She'd run from him. And despite the small size of the town, she'd managed to avoid him for weeks after their night together. When he finally saw her again, in the parking lot of the grocery store of all places, she'd quickly stuffed her packages in her car and peeled out of the parking lot.

If it had meant nothing to her, why in the hell had she run?

"You can lie to yourself all you want to," he whispered softly. "But that night wasn't just about sex, and you damn well know it."

"Please, just stop it, Sawyer. Stop trying to make it more than it was." She stared at him, her expression resolved. "You were hurting. You needed comfort. I decided to provide it. It was a pity fu—"

"Don't you dare," he cut her off. He crowded her, invading every inch of her space. "Don't ever reduce what happened between us to some pity screw." He pointed to his chest. "I was there. I *felt* it. I felt the way you shivered in my arms. I felt the way your body clenched mine, the way you clung to me as if it would kill you to let go. That had nothing to do with pity."

Her chest expanded with the deep breath she inhaled as her eyes fell shut.

Sawyer captured her chin in his hand and tipped her face up. "It was more than just sex, Paxton. You know it was."

When she opened her eyes they were filled with accusation. "So why did you marry someone else?"

Sawyer dropped his hand. The hurt in her eyes knocked the breath from his lungs, as if it were a physical blow. He took several steps back, his hands falling to his sides.

"Why?" she repeated. "If that night was more than just a pity screw, if it was this magical experience we shared, why did you marry someone else just a few months later, Sawyer?" She sucked in a deep breath before she asked in a pained whisper, "Were the two of you engaged when we slept together?"

"No." Sawyer shook his head. He ran his palm down his face, suddenly hating everything about this conversation.

"Angelique and I were…" He paused, unsure how to explain his marriage without sounding like a cold, indifferent jerk.

The problem was that his marriage *had* been cold and indifferent. It had been a mistake from the start, a complete mockery of that sacred institution.

If he explained it to her, would Paxton understand just why he did it, or would it make him look even worse in her eyes? Sawyer realized that he didn't have a choice. At the very least, he owed her this explanation.

"Angelique and I didn't have much of an engagement," he started. He shoved his hands into his pockets and backed up against the beam he'd rested on earlier, knocking a couple of dead leaves from the arbor's vines. "We didn't have much of a marriage at all, if you want to know the full truth." He looked up at Paxton and found her watching him with a rapt, curious gaze.

"I married Angelique because it's what was expected of me," Sawyer said. "It's what my dad wanted. It's what her dad had wanted."

"You make it sound like an arranged marriage."

He shrugged. "In a way that's exactly what it was. Our families have been friends for years. Our dads grew up in the same neighborhood in New Orleans, one of the roughest in the city. They both beat the odds and made a better life for themselves, and they remained best friends through it all. Angelique and I both attended Tulane together. We dated for about a year back in college, and although we knew we weren't compatible, our dads both thought it was a foregone conclusion that we would eventually marry.

"Her dad was killed in a private plane crash about ten years ago. He never got to see us married. When my dad got sick, we decided to just do it because we knew it would make him happy."

"You married someone you didn't love to make your father happy?"

"It worked," Sawyer said. "At least for the last month or so that he was alive to see it."

"But you stayed married for three years."

His brow rose. "You were keeping tabs on me?"

Her expression turned sarcastic. "This is a frighteningly small town, Sawyer. You can't help but learn other people's business."

"Very true," he said with a humorless laugh.

"So?" she asked. "Why did you stay married if you didn't love her?"

He hunched his shoulders. "It was convenient. I know that makes us sound like the most unromantic couple in the world, but it's the truth. Angelique accepted a job with the public defenders office in Chicago at the same time that the Army Corps transferred me to Illinois. We were more like roommates than husband and wife. In the first year or so we were both too busy in our new jobs to recognize what was missing from our lives, but then Angelique met someone who she actually cared for."

"That sounds…horrible for you," she said.

"Not really. The day she took me out to dinner to tell me, all I felt was relief. I was happy for her. She's a good person. She deserved to find someone to make her happy."

"So do you."

"That's why I came back to Gauthier instead of returning to my house in New Orleans," he said. "But then I discovered that the one person I wanted—the woman I believed could make me happy—had moved away."

Several moments passed between them. Sawyer pushed away from the beam and walked over to her again.

"You felt something for me that night, Paxton. It may have started out of pity, but that's not the way it ended. You left because you were as shocked by what we both experienced as I was." He cupped her chin again. "All I'm asking for is a chance."

A shuddery breath escaped her lips. She glided her fingers along the nape of his neck, then cradled the back of his head, pulling him closer to her.

"It scares the hell out of me," she admitted. "But maybe…maybe we can see how it goes. How's that for taking a chance?"

A subtle smile drew across Sawyer's lips. "That's a good start." His lips drifted across hers. "But this is an even better one."

"Exactly why am I helping you make apple butter during my lunch break?" Paxton asked as she plucked another Red Delicious from the bag Shayla had bought at the new farmer's market in Saint Pierre.

"Because it's a healthier alternative to regular butter or cream cheese as a spread for pastries," she said. "I'm thinking of maybe canning it and selling jars at the Jazzy Bean if I can get the recipe just right."

"That health-conscious menu is still working for you?"

"Absolutely," her friend said. "Didn't you see the chart

on the community board I keep above the condiment bar? A bunch of my regulars have a fitness contest going on right now. They're trying to lose a thousand pounds as a group by next year's Founder's Day Celebration." She sent Paxton a cheeky grin. "I would say 'I told you so' since you were one of my biggest doubters, but I'm much too nice for that."

"That is so not fair," Paxton said. "I never doubted *you*. It's the people in this town that I doubted. You know most of them are stuck in their ways."

"Well, I'm changing their ways one Zumba class at a time," Shayla said.

When Shayla returned to Gauthier to open her own coffee shop after working in the coffee industry in Seattle for years, Paxton thought it was both bold and brave but also the tiniest bit crazy. And when Shayla decided that the Jazzy Bean would only serve heart-healthy food items, Paxton was certain that her friend's grand ideas would go down in a blaze of glory.

She had been proven wrong. And she couldn't be happier about it.

Shayla had turned the Jazzy Bean into the kind of place that people from neighboring towns drove out of their way to visit. Her friend was a marketing genius, which helped tremendously. In addition to great coffee, pastries and café-style food offerings, the Jazzy Bean also hosted Zumba classes three nights a week and live jazz music on the weekends. It was, without a doubt, one of the best success stories to come out of the revitalization of downtown Gauthier.

"I heard the Jazzy Bean was packed last Friday night," Paxton said. "Did the high school's jazz ensemble earn enough money for their trip to Washington?"

"They're getting close," Shayla said. "They're going to perform again in a couple of weeks. Oh, did I tell you I landed Simone Thibodaux? She's debuting her new album at the Jazzy Bean."

"Seriously?" Paxton said. The performer was the daughter of famed jazz singer Madeline Thibodaux, whose French Quarter jazz club, Maddie's Spot, had just been named the hottest new club in New Orleans by a local magazine. It was a huge feat for a city with an endless number of hot spots. "Will she be performing before I leave at the end of the month?"

Shayla shook her head. "Nope. You'll just have to stick around longer."

"Or I can just go to Maddie's Spot and see her," Paxton pointed out.

"But you would be so plagued with guilt for not supporting her show at the Jazzy Bean that you wouldn't be able to enjoy yourself."

Paxton's head flew back with her laugh. "All joking aside, landing Simone Thibodaux is huge. Have I mentioned how proud I am of you?"

"Only a dozen times since you've been back," Shayla said. "You're slipping."

"Well, I'll say it again. I am so proud of you. I didn't think Gauthier was big enough to sustain a coffee shop like the Jazzy Bean, and I am so happy that you've proven me wrong."

"Aww." Shayla set her paring knife on the counter, ran to Paxton's side of the kitchen island and wrapped her arms around her. "I haven't forgiven you for moving to Little Rock, but I'm still proud of the work you're doing, too." She gave Paxton an extra squeeze before returning to her side of the counter.

"How is the project going, by the way?" Shayla asked. "You said Sawyer had to go into his office at the Army Corps this afternoon, right? Why didn't you go with him?"

"It has to do with whatever project he was working on before they transferred him to this one."

"So, how is yours going?" Shayla asked again.

Paxton released a sigh. "How much truth do you want?"

Shayla's hand stilled with her paring knife hovering above the red-skinned apple she'd started to peel.

"What's wrong?" Shayla asked. "You all found something bad, didn't you? Is all of Gauthier poised to drown during the next big rainstorm?"

"It's nothing like that."

"Be honest with me, Pax. I've got a lot invested in this town. So does Xavier. He's been turning down offers left and right in order to stay here and run the clinic."

Shayla's husband, Xavier Wright, was an implant from Atlanta. He'd come to the hospital in Maplesville to work as an ER doctor in conjunction with a program that supplied medical personnel to underserved areas. During his stint at Maplesville General, Matthew Gauthier had convinced Xavier to volunteer a few hours a week at a clinic that Matt had opened for low-income residents. Shayla had convinced Xavier to stay for life.

"Is Xavier seriously considering other offers?" Paxton asked, suddenly troubled by the thought of Shayla leaving. Which was a bit cheeky on her part, since she was the one who had left first.

Shayla put her mind at ease with a casual wave of her hand. "Not really," she said. "He gets them, but he's more than settled where he is. Besides, he could never leave Kristi and Cass."

"Well, that's good to know," Paxton said. "What Xavier does helps a lot of people here. And you don't have to worry about Gauthier drowning in a flood. We're going to get that system in place in time."

"So, what's the issue?"

"Do you remember those flood maps I mentioned Monday?" Paxton asked.

"The ones Sawyer thought were outdated?"

Paxton nodded. "The rest of the team at Bolt-Myer agreed that we need to study the topography of the landscape before we move forward. Thankfully, it won't set us back too much schedule-wise, but this will be the first project I've ever managed that will come in behind schedule."

"Maybe you all can make up for lost time on the back end," Shayla said. "Although coming in a little late doesn't sound like a big deal if it means the flood protection system will be done right. It needs to be done right."

With a sly smile tilting up the corner of her mouth as she mixed up a pungent combination of ground cloves and nutmeg, Shayla asked, "So how have *other* things been going?"

"Meaning?"

She picked up the paring knife and pointed it at Paxton. "Don't you play dumb with me, girl. I know there has to be something going on. I could have baked croissants with the heat I felt between you and Sawyer on Monday. I want the dirt."

Paxton closed her eyes and released a frustrated sigh. "He has me climbing the walls."

"Hold. Up!" Shayla shrieked. "He has you *climbing*

the walls or he has you up *against* the walls, as in… you know."

Paxton opened her eyes and rolled them so hard at her best friend that she nearly gave herself a headache.

"Okay, okay, no having you up against the wall yet, but it sounds like progress is being made. It's about time," Shayla said, going back to her apple peeling. "I knew Sawyer would step up his game now that he's got you in that tiny conference room all day."

Paxton pushed the bowl to the side and dropped her head onto the silicon cutting board. She thumped it several times, groaning like a wounded animal.

She finally looked up at Shayla and said in a pathetically annoying voice that she only used when at her whiniest, "I don't know what to do."

"First thing to do is get this piece of apple from the middle of your forehead." Shayla reached over and plucked the apple away. "And what's so hard for you to figure out? Sawyer is a great catch, Pax. In fact, if you asked just about any single woman in town, he's *the* catch."

"You've been knowing me for how long now?" Paxton asked, her brow arching. "You haven't figured out yet that I'm not like the other single women in this town and never have been?"

It was Shayla's turn to indulge in the frustrated sigh, but of course hers was twice as dramatic.

"Forgive me, I forgot you're Miss I Don't Need a Man on My Arm."

"Actually, Miss Independent is a shorter and much more accurate description."

"Whatever," Shayla said. "But even Miss Independent has to admit there are worse things than having the hots for Sawyer Robertson, especially after you finally realized that he's had the hots for you all this time." Shayla shook her head. "I still can't believe you didn't know."

"Can we stop talking about how clueless I am for a moment?"

"If you want my opinion," Shayla said, speaking right over her. "You need to stop holding out and get you some. It's good for the complexion. See?" She ran her hand along her jaw as if she were showcasing a prize on *The Price Is Right*.

"Thanks for the advice, but I get quite enough to keep my skin clear," Paxton argued.

"Uh, I don't think so. Your coworker in Little Rock doesn't count. That was months ago, and you told me that you nearly fell asleep in the middle of it."

Paxton grimaced. "I tell you too much about my sex life."

"True, which is how I know that you haven't gotten any in a while."

"I—"

Shayla held up a finger. "Vibrators don't count."

"Depends on the brand you use," Paxton countered, sticking her tongue out at her.

"Would you just admit it already," Shayla said. "You're at least a little curious about what Sawyer has to offer when the lights go out. You have to be."

Actually, she wasn't curious. She didn't have to be because she already knew exactly what Sawyer had to offer. They'd done it with the lights *on*.

Paxton was not looking forward to Shayla going ballistic over her keeping her one-night stand with Sawyer a secret from her. The thought sent an unsettling barrage of questions parading through her mind.

Why hadn't she told Shayla about Sawyer? The two of them had shared details about every single guy they had ever been with—even the questionable characters they'd given their goodies to during their wild college years. But when it came to that one night with Sawyer, Paxton just couldn't bring herself to share it.

Shayla reached over and tapped her on the arm. "Just remember what I said before. Sawyer is one of the good guys. Don't let your typical hang-ups get in the way of it this time. Give him a chance."

"What are my typical hang-ups?" Paxton asked, a fair amount of affront in her voice.

Shayla didn't hesitate to point them out.

"You believe everyone judges you because of how you grew up, so you turn around and judge them. Usually unfairly. And especially when it comes to Sawyer. You've always unfairly judged him."

"Wow," Paxton said with a snort. "Don't hold back. Tell me what you really think."

"I finally am," Shayla said. "I should have told you long before this, because I love you like a sister. Like a damn twin." Shayla covered her forearm again. "No one cares that you grew up in a trailer behind Harlon's Bar. No one cares that the jerk who provided the other half of your DNA never claimed you as his. None of that matters, Pax. It definitely doesn't matter to Sawyer. It never has."

Paxton pulled her bottom lip between her teeth. "I just... I don't know," she said. "These last couple of days have been really good, Shayla. I'm just not used to this."

"Not used to what?"

"Being with a guy like this. Just hanging out together, getting to know each other. Did you know he was awarded the highest honor that a civilian can be honored with by the Army Corps for his work after Hurricane Katrina? And he donated a huge amount of money to the animal shelter. Oh, *and* back when he first moved to New Orleans after he finished college, he started mentoring two young boys at a school in the Ninth Ward. Those two boys just finished college this year. One is even going to medical school."

"Sounds like the two of you *are* getting to know each other. And you now see the kind of man Sawyer is, right?"

"I do," Paxton said, still nervously pulling on her lower lip. "I just don't know what to do with any of this." She looked up at Shayla. "I'm not used to it being so easy. I just keep waiting for the other shoe to drop."

"Forget the other shoe! Sometimes it really is this easy, Pax. Not every guy is a jerk. And Sawyer has never been that kind of guy, even though all the ingredients are there. He's rich and popular and could be the biggest jerk ever, but he has always had this huge heart."

"So maybe I should just see where this leads?"

"Hell yes!" Shayla said. "No more questioning it. Just go with it. Let that man take you up against the wall so you can come back and tell me all about it." Shayla pointed the paring knife at her again. "And you better tell me as soon as the orgasm wears off, or I swear I'll cut you."

"I really do tell you too much about my damn sex life." Paxton reached for another apple, but Shayla snatched the bowl out of her way. "Hey, give that back. I'm here to help you, remember?"

"You take off too much flesh when you peel. The

whole helping me make apple butter thing was only a ruse to get you here, anyway."

Paxton's eyes narrowed. "What kind of no good are you up to, devil woman?"

"Come to the game tonight," Shayla said.

Paxton put her hands up and slid from the stool. "Forget it."

"Oh, come on, Pax. It'll be fun."

"What is with this town and high school football games?"

"The same thing that's with every small Southern town when it comes to Friday night high school football. It's a religion. And don't use your mom's place as an excuse. Most of the town will be at the game. Belinda and Jessie will be able to handle the handful of people who might drop in at the bar. If you want, you can even leave at the end of the third quarter so you can get to the bar in time to help with the postgame rush."

"Wanting to help out at the bar has nothing to do with why I don't want to go to the game," Paxton said. "It's not my thing, Shayla. It never has been."

"Because you never gave it a chance back in high school. It's going to be fun."

Paxton slanted her friend a look. "For who?"

"Please," Shayla said. "Do it for me?"

"Ugh," she grunted. "You're such a pain in the ass."

"But you love me, anyway." Shayla blew her a kiss. "Meet me back here at seven. We'll ride together."

"I need to get back to the office," Paxton said as she grabbed her purse and headed for the door. "I'll think about the game," she said over her shoulder.

Ever the smart-ass, Shayla said, "See you at seven!"

Chapter 8

Bright stadium lights illuminated the perfectly manicured field at Gauthier High School, reflecting off the ferocious lion logo holding center stage in the middle of the field. The chain-link fence surrounding the stadium was covered in hand-painted signs promising to "Manhandle the Mustangs" and "Bring Home the Iron Boot."

Homecoming was always the biggest game of the season, and tonight's game had even more at stake, as it pitted the Gauthier Lions against their archrivals, the Maplesville Mustangs. The game had become a yearly tradition, with the victor winning the honor of displaying the coveted iron trophy in the shape of a boot—representing the shape of Louisiana—at the school for the remainder of the academic year.

There was not a single seat left in the stands. People were crowded at least three deep along the fence, as well.

Shayla was right; it looked as if every single person in Gauthier and Maplesville was at this game tonight.

Paxton buried her chin inside her jacket collar and braced herself against the blast of cold wind that blew across the bleachers. A collective *whooooa* went through the crowd.

People north of the Mason-Dixon would probably laugh at the crowd's reaction to the temperature, which was just under fifty degrees, but south Louisianans weren't used to such weather, especially this early in the season. The October cold front that had blown in had everyone pulling out their winter gear.

"Fun, right?" Shayla said as she sat next to Paxton and handed her a hot chocolate from the concession stand.

"If I had a list of things that are more fun than this, it would stretch from here all the way back to Little Rock," Paxton answered.

"Well, can you pretend it's fun so I don't feel guilty for dragging you here?"

"I want you to feel guilty," she said, taking a sip of her hot chocolate. She grimaced. "This is horrible."

"I know. It's instant. But it's not supposed to taste good—it's just supposed to warm you up." Shayla nudged her shoulder and pointed to the far end of the football field. "The homecoming court is about to take their pregame walk."

"And what is that?" Paxton asked.

"Just watch it," Shayla said.

All of this was so foreign to her, Paxton was at a complete loss about how to act.

Back when they were in high school, she attended exactly two football games during her entire four years as a student, and neither of them had been the homecoming game. Not only did she abhor all the silly pageantry that appeared to her to be nothing more than a chance to heap more praise on the popular crowd, but she also hated football.

She really could think of a million places she'd rather be right now. She'd probably spend the majority of her time tonight coming up with a mental list. It would be better than having to pay attention to the game or to the homecoming court, which was currently receiving a standing ovation from the crowd.

She snorted.

A standing ovation? For what? Knowing how to walk in heels and wave at the same time?

Stop it! she mentally chastised herself.

Paxton slunk deeper into her collar, ashamed at the petty thoughts swirling through her head. These were kids, for goodness' sake. And she was no longer that girl she once was in high school, seething with jealousy, coveting her fellow classmates' fun-filled, carefree lives.

That Paxton Jones, the girl who had never fit into celebrations like this one, was gone. She had been replaced by the self-assured woman who was successful enough to buy her mother a bar and wear designer clothes and do all those other things she couldn't do back in high school.

This new Paxton could put up with a few hours of this spectacle for her friend's sake, couldn't she?

The homecoming court walked the length of the football field. It looked rather silly to see the girls in their fancy dresses while their escorts—all football players— wore their uniforms. But since no one else pointed out the ridiculousness of it, Paxton decided it was best to keep her opinion to herself.

Once the girls were seated on the dais that had been

erected on the running track that surrounded the field, their escorts joined the other members of the team underneath the goalpost at the far end of the field.

After the team ran through the sign the cheerleaders held up for them, everyone stood for the playing of the national anthem by the Gauthier Lions marching band. A small contingent from each team walked arm in arm to the center of the field for the coin toss, with a roar erupting when the Lions won the toss.

The moment the Mustangs' kicker sent the ball sailing into the air, Paxton lost all interest in what was taking place on the field. While the two teams battled it out during the first quarter, she read through her work email on her phone, replying to those she'd flagged as low-priority follow-ups throughout the week. She shook the green-and-white pom-pom shaker Shayla had shoved into her hand when she heard the crowd cheer and joined in with the booing when that reaction was warranted.

The only time she raised her head was when Xavier arrived. She gave him a quick hug, then went back to checking her email.

"You could have stayed home for this," Shayla told her at the end of the first quarter.

Paxton looked up from her phone. "What?"

Shayla grabbed her pant leg. "They're calling out the classes by decade. You have to stand and cheer when they call the decade that you graduated."

"Seriously?" Paxton said.

They called the 1990s.

"Come on!" Shayla grabbed her by the elbow and hauled her up. Paxton shook the pom-pom as enthusiastically as she could muster, which wasn't much at all.

"You really do suck at this school spirit thing," Shayla

said as they wedged back into their spots in the packed bleachers.

"Again, how long have you known me?"

Shayla rolled her eyes. "At halftime they're going to call each year individually, so you'll have to stand again."

"Oh, joy," Paxton said.

"It's Alumni Night. The whole point is to honor alumni. The football players from each class get to walk on the field and get a little taste of those glory days. It's fun."

For someone who actually had fun back in high school. But Paxton refrained from pointing that out.

She actually started to feel bad over her lack of enthusiasm. She knew Shayla was only trying to make her feel as if she were a part of the bigger group, just as she had in high school. The least she could do was pretend she was enjoying herself, for her friend's sake.

Determined to abandon her stank attitude, Paxton tucked her phone away and tried her hardest to pay attention to the game. It was a stretch, but when the largest player on the Lions' defense—who had to weigh at least three hundred pounds—recovered a fumble on the Mustangs' fifteen yard line and ran it in for a touchdown, even Paxton had to stand up and cheer. There was a ten-minute delay while the paramedics rolled out an oxygen tank for the player, who had winded himself so much with the fifteen-yard run that he couldn't even make it back to the sidelines.

While the player was being tended to, her eyes roamed the rest of the field. Paxton spotted a cadre of men and women in letterman jackets congregating on the sidelines around the thirty-yard line. She realized it must be the alumni taking part in the halftime ceremony Shayla had mentioned, players and cheerleaders from years past.

Her eyes sought Sawyer. He wasn't hard to pick out of the crowd. As one of the Gauthier Lions' most decorated quarterbacks of all time, he was the very center of attention, with fellow players giving him hearty pats on the back and the cheerleaders sidling up to him with unabashed adoration in their eyes.

Paxton was hit with a wave of nostalgia that was both unsettling and, in an odd way she didn't quite understand, comforting.

Standing on those sidelines was the Sawyer of her teenage daydreams, the tall, strapping, handsome boy who was revered by everyone who knew him. Seeing him there in his green-and-white letterman jacket, surrounded by his adoring fans, conjured up so many past memories that Paxton had to remind herself to take a breath.

All too soon that odd comfort she'd felt was overcome by a rush of dark unease. As she stared at the former cheerleaders and players encircling him, all of those old insecurities that had plagued her back in high school came flooding back. Some of those people currently worshipping Sawyer right now were the same people who used to look down on her.

And despite what her best friend thought, her *hangups* were not a figment of her imagination. Hell, it wasn't until Shayla had befriended her that anyone had even bothered to acknowledge her at all.

To so many of the people in these stands, she was nothing more than Belinda Jones's illegitimate daughter. She was the girl who had to work in Harlon's just to help her family get by, the girl who made the same jeans last for three years because she was too proud to accept hand-me-downs. The girl who never fit in at high school games or pep rallies or homecoming dances.

The girl who didn't belong here.

Paxton's chest tightened to the point that she could barely take a breath.

At that moment, Sawyer looked into the stands, and their eyes locked. He smiled and gave her a little wave, but all Paxton could see was the bounty of reasons why they didn't fit together—why they would never fit. They were both from this small town, but they were from two different worlds. And she didn't belong in his. She never would.

She had to get out of there.

Paxton caught Shayla's arm to get her attention and said, "I'm going to the restroom. I'll be back."

"Okay," she called. "Don't take too long or you'll miss when they call our graduating year."

Paxton nodded, even though it would take an army to make her come back into these stands. She jogged down the stadium steps to the path below, which traveled underneath the bleachers to the stadium exit.

"Paxton! Pax, wait up!"

She turned, stunned to see Sawyer jogging up behind her.

"What are you doing here?" Paxton asked. "Aren't you supposed to take to the field in a few minutes?"

"I was, until I saw you leaving. Where are you going?"

She shook her head. "I don't belong here, Sawyer. I don't know why I let Shayla drag me to this game."

"Paxton—"

"Don't." She put her hand up. "Don't feed me lines about how I belong here just as much as everyone else does, or any of that other crap."

His deep chuckle came as such a surprise that Paxton jerked back a step. "What's so funny?"

"You," he said without hesitation, without one ounce of remorse. "You're so clueless that it's actually comical."

Yet another person calling her clueless today.

Before she could retaliate, he took her by the arm and tugged her deeper beneath the bleachers, away from the concrete path leading to the parking lot. Splotches of the gleaming stadium lights filtered through the stands, illuminating people here and there, mostly teen couples making out.

Sawyer positioned her against the steel leg truss. Gripping the metal above her head with one hand, he caught her chin with the other and nudged her face up. Instead of pissing her off, the humor sparkling in his eyes made her want to smile, too. But she fought the urge. Just barely.

"Paxton, do you have any idea how often I sought Shayla out in the stands back when we were in school, hoping that she had somehow convinced you to come with her to a game?"

She blinked hard, dumbfounded by his admission. "Why? You played in front of packed stadiums every Friday night. I remember the frenzy surrounding you back in our senior year. People who had never heard of Gauthier before would travel from as far as Covington and Picayune to come see you play."

"I didn't care about those people. You're the one I wanted to impress."

"But why? I didn't even like football. I still don't."

He shrugged. "Nothing else I tried to do ever got your attention. I thought maybe if I impressed you with my football skills, you'd finally notice me."

"I noticed you," Paxton said before she could even think to hold the words back.

The crazy-sexy smile that gradually lifted the corners of his mouth did unbelievable things to her insides.

"You did a damn fine job of pretending that you didn't." His eyes roamed her face, his fingers brushing her cheekbone.

He leaned forward, his breath skimming along the sensitive skin of her neck. "You want to know a secret?"

Paxton sucked in a deep breath. Swallowed. Then nodded.

"When we would fall behind, I would pretend that you *were* there," he whispered into her ear. "Coach Jackson may have thought it was his pep talks that got me going, but it wasn't. I would pretend you were in the stands, watching me, and it was all the encouragement I needed to turn the game around.

"So, even though you weren't there, I still owe that senior season to you. Because just the thought of you was enough to make me want to be better."

Her heart flipped twice, did a waltz and then collapsed in flat-out exhaustion from the tailspin his sweetly whispered words induced.

She tried to avert her eyes, but he wouldn't let her.

"Now tell me," he said. "Why were you really leaving?"

"I already told you. Because I never fit in here. And…" She shook her head. God, if she started to cry she would never, ever forgive herself. She didn't cry. Especially here of all places. "Seeing all of you on that field tonight—the cheerleaders, the homecoming queen— it just reminded me of how much I don't belong." She looked up at him, and as much as she tried, she couldn't mask the hurt in her voice. "I was never that girl, Sawyer."

He leaned in so close that their heads nearly touched. With his intense eyes locking hold on her gaze, he said, "You were *always* that girl for me."

Paxton went liquid as a warmth she'd never experienced before embraced her, wrapping her up in a blanket of sheer enchantment.

"You know what I just realized?" Sawyer whispered, trailing his lips along her jawline. "I can finally live out a fantasy I've had since high school."

"What fantasy?" she asked.

"To kiss a girl under the bleachers."

Sensations in all makes and models fluttered through her stomach as his strong fingers gently gripped her waist.

"In four years of high school you never kissed a girl beneath the bleachers?" Paxton asked, her voice thready. She was trying her hardest not to gasp. "Isn't that like a rite of passage or something?"

"The only girl I wanted to kiss beneath the bleachers was never at the games. But since she's here now, it's only fair that I get to kiss her."

Her heartbeat escalated as Sawyer's mouth closed in on her, his lips slanting over hers.

"Eww, gross," came a teenage voice from somewhere in the darkness. "Let's get out of here. I'm not here to see some old couple making out."

Paxton nearly backed away from the kiss so she could

tell the kid off for calling them old, but when Sawyer's wet tongue started a hot trail along the seam of her lips she forgot teenagers even existed. She forgot about everything but the man whose splayed hand was slowly making its way up her spine. He pulled her closer, and the telling bulge pressing against her stomach told Paxton all she needed to know about how incredibly turned on he was.

He wasn't the only one.

A roar erupted above them, and the bleachers shook with the crowd's rowdy cheers, but Paxton could not care less about whatever was happening above their heads or on the field. Apparently, neither could Sawyer. He never lost stride as he parted her lips and found his way inside.

Paxton closed her eyes and soaked in this moment as her girlhood dreams were brought to life within Sawyer's arms. Back and forth her tongue moved in rhythm with his, rediscovering his texture, his taste. She moved her hand inside his letterman jacket, trailing them along his sides before settling them at his waist.

Sawyer narrowed the distance between them even more, his big, solid body pressing against hers as his tongue delved deeper, the gentle yet sure thrusts awakening those same feelings she'd experienced when he kissed her in the arbor. Paxton moved her hand to the back of his head and held him in place. She sucked his tongue, wanting it, *needing* it to fill her mouth. Her entire being grabbed hungrily at this small glimpse of heaven on earth.

"Okay, you two. Break it up."

She and Sawyer both jumped and pulled apart at the strictly spoken command.

Zoe Taylor, who had been a senior and student body

president during their freshman year, and who had just been hired as the new assistant principal at Gauthier High, crossed her arms over her chest and cleared her throat.

"Really?" she said. "I expected better from the two of you." Then a smile curved up the corners of her lips as she winked and walked away.

"I can't believe we got caught kissing under the bleachers by the principal," Paxton said.

"I think that's another of those rites of passage. We're hitting it out of the ballpark tonight."

"I'll check it off my bucket list as soon as I get home."

His deep chuckle caused goose bumps to pop up all along her skin. Or maybe those were the lingering effects of that kiss. Paxton had a feeling she would be experiencing those for the rest of the week.

"Do you still want to leave?" Sawyer asked.

She pulled her bottom lip between her teeth and nodded. "I do. I just don't like football."

He put a hand over his heart. "You're killing me, Pax."

She laughed. "Sorry."

He smoothed his hand up her arm and to her neck, fitting the back of her head in his palm and brushing his thumb back and forth along the pulse point behind her ear.

"Would you mind if I walked you to your car?"

She frowned. "Actually, I don't have a car. Shayla was my ride."

One brow arched quizzically. "So how exactly were you planning on getting home?"

"I guess I hadn't thought that far ahead."

A low, deep laugh rumbled from his chest yet again. Paxton would be annoyed with him if she didn't find the sound so sexy. He caught her by both hands and started to walk backward.

"Where are we going?"

"I'll drive you to your mom's."

Paxton stopped short. "But don't you want to stay for the rest of the game?"

He shook his head. "I've had my time on the field as a Gauthier Fighting Lion." He pulled her in closer. "Besides, I'm hoping I can convince you to take a detour."

Her stomach did that flipping thing again.

"Where are you looking to take me?" she asked.

His brow hitched.

Oh, she was *so* there.

"Oh, my God! This is so good." The moan that escaped her lips drizzled down Sawyer's spine.

"I told you it would be," he replied.

"It's been so long since I had it. I just didn't think it could still be this good."

"It's always as good as the first time."

Paxton let out a satisfied sigh and sat back in the chair she'd occupied for the past hour on his rear deck. As she licked her fingers clean of the sticky remnants of the roasted marshmallow she'd just eaten, Sawyer had to stop himself from going for her lips. He wouldn't move too fast.

But he *would* make his move tonight.

He threw another log into the built-in fire bowl that he'd never used once since moving into this house. It was only fitting that he christen it with Paxton. Picturing the two of them spending countless nights together like this had become his new favorite pastime over the past hour.

She reached for another marshmallow, speared it with a kebab spear and placed it over the fire bowl.

"Here," Sawyer said, handing her the one he'd been roasting for several minutes.

Paxton stared at the slightly charred marshmallow. "You're giving me your marshmallow?" she asked. The awe in her voice made him wonder what the other men in her life had ever done for her.

"I will roast as many marshmallows as your heart desires," Sawyer said. "I just have to warn you, you'll probably get sick after the seventh or eight one."

Her head flew back with her rich laugh. "Now *that* I do remember, but my mom always had seltzer water or ginger ale on hand."

"So this really was a thing?" he said. "You and your mom really roasted marshmallows when you were a kid?"

Her enthusiastic nod combined with that bright smile was infectious. Sawyer couldn't help but smile himself.

"She used to take me camping in the yard, that patch of land between our trailer and Harlon's Bar," she clarified. "We'd roast marshmallows and she'd tell me ghost stories and we'd read books that I picked up from the library. I guess it was her version of a low-cost vacation, because she could never afford the time off from work or the money it would take to go on a real one."

Sawyer thought about his own childhood and couldn't deny the stark difference to hers. Because his father had been sequestered in his Ninth Ward neighborhood while growing up, he'd vowed that his son would get out and see the world. Sawyer had visited more than a dozen states by the time he was twelve. He'd been to the top of the Empire State Building, observed the majestic beauty of the Grand Canyon and dipped his toes into the Pacific Ocean off the coast of California.

"It's okay, Sawyer," she said. He looked up at her. "I know what you're thinking, and, really, it's okay."

He doubted she knew what he was thinking, and Sawyer wasn't inclined to share his true thoughts with her. Not right now. He didn't want the startling difference between the way they grew up creating any more of a chasm between them, especially tonight.

"I was just thinking—" he started, but she cut him off.

"You were thinking about all the cool places you've visited, but you're afraid to say anything because you think it will make me feel bad."

Damn. Maybe his poker face wasn't as good as he thought it was.

She held the marshmallow she'd been roasting out to him.

"Okay, yeah. That is kind of what I was thinking," Sawyer said before taking a bite. A trail of the warm sticky substance fell onto his chin.

"Don't," she said. "Those campouts with my mom are some of my very best memories. I didn't need anything else. I'm ashamed to admit just how jealous I was of some of the things other kids in Gauthier—those whose families had money—got to do, but fancy vacations was never one of them.

"And it's not as if I was stuck in Gauthier my entire childhood, either. When Shayla and Braylon were kids, they would go to the beach in Biloxi for a week every summer. Their folks were sweet enough to bring me along. So, you see. There's no reason for you to feel bad for me."

She reached over and ran her thumb along his chin where the marshmallow had fallen. Her eyes zeroed in on his lips. "You missed a spot."

The husky rasp coloring her words clutched at his gut. And lower.

"That was the best way you could think of to clean it off?" Sawyer asked.

Her brow lifted, a slow smile edging up the corner of her mouth. "What exactly do you suggest?"

He shrugged. "It all depends."

"On what?"

Sawyer leaned forward. "On whether you plan to sneak away like you did the last time," he said, his voice as husky as hers.

Her gaze traveled from his mouth up to his eyes. "There's a lot I want to do tonight, but leaving isn't a part of the plan."

Sawyer closed the distance between them. "Then why in the hell are you not doing it?"

He wrapped his arms around her and lifted her out of the chair, settling her legs around his waist. Her lips collided with his, thick with passion, heavy with the lust the two of them had been fighting over these past couple of weeks. With her body wrapped around him, Sawyer started for the open French doors. Once inside he laid her on the chaise lounge in the living room and quickly covered her body with his.

"Pax, do you know how many times I dream about doing this every day?"

He charged for that spot on her neck just below her ear. Three years had passed, yet he still remembered how much she'd loved it when he sucked there. Sawyer went for it again, first sucking, then gently biting, while his hands roamed the soft skin underneath her shirt.

She released a low moan, her neck arching, reaching for his teeth and his tongue.

"I want you so much," she admitted in a rush of breath.

Her words, spoken in that lusty, desperate voice, had the effect of throwing hot grease on a burning fire. Sawyer's body went up in flames.

He kissed his way down her body, then buried his head underneath her shirt, kissing his way back up again as he rolled the shirt up and off her. The bra came next, going the way of her shirt.

For a moment Sawyer just hovered above her, his body temporarily stunned at how sexy she looked dressed in nothing but skintight jeans. He needed her fully naked, but there was something so sensual, so damn sexy about half of her body being bared to him, that he just needed to soak it in for a minute.

Then he decided a minute was too long.

He hooked his hands in the waistband of her jeans and peeled them from her body, quickly removing her satin panties after that.

Sawyer pulled her to the edge of the chaise and knelt on the floor before her. He was overwhelmed by the feelings swirling within him as his eyes roved over her body. This woman had captured his heart so long ago. Nothing would make him happier than finally having the chance to give it to her.

Actually, right now, he saw one thing that could make him pretty happy. Running his palms up her inner thighs, he spread her legs apart and hooked them over his shoulders.

He was like a starving man who had just had a banquet feast fit for a king set before him. As much as he was dying to pounce on her body with a rapaciousness unparalleled to anything he'd experienced before, Sawyer told himself to take it slow.

He made his way up the inside of her thigh, marking the ridiculously soft skin with gentle love bites. He soothed each bite with a soft kiss and followed with a slow, wet lick. He kissed his way around her, deliberately avoiding the one place he knew she wanted him the most.

"Sawyer!" Paxton yelled. "Stop teasing me."

But teasing her was exactly what he wanted to do. He drew the backs of his fingers along her inner thigh, then around her center before finally giving her some relief. Using the pad of his thumb, he lightly teased the mass of nerves at her cleft, then rolled it between his fingers. Paxton rocked her hips, her body jerking as soft whimpers escaped her lips. Sawyer grew harder with every moan, but he fought the urge to strip out of his own clothes and fill her body with his. Right now it was all about her pleasure. He wanted to make it so good that she would never think about leaving his bed again.

Tucking his hands underneath her, he gripped her ass and lifted her body to his mouth.

That first taste on his tongue gave him new life.

Sawyer forgot all about her pleasure and selfishly concentrated on his as he explored the exquisite world between her legs. Her slick, tender flesh tasted even better than he remembered. He buried his face between her thighs, closing his mouth over her center and sucking hard. He flicked his tongue back and forth over the tight bud at her cleft, branding it as his.

He felt Paxton's thighs quivering around his head

moments before her back bowed and her scream tore through the room.

With a promise to himself that he would return to tasting the deliciousness between her legs, Sawyer stood and quickly got rid of his clothes. He couldn't wait any longer.

Covering himself with the condom he'd taken earlier from his bedroom, Sawyer fitted himself between her thighs and entered her with one long, deep thrust. Pleasure, pure and explosive, burst throughout his being as he found heaven. Nothing in this world had ever come close to the way it felt when Paxton gripped his body. It was as if she was made exclusively for him.

With a desperation that had his limbs shaking, Sawyer gripped her hips and pumped in and out, quickly becoming addicted to the way her inner muscles clutched him as he slid deeper, then retreated. The sensation of being engulfed in her incredible heat was like a drug, flooding his brain with the most erotic pleasure he had ever experienced.

"You feel...so good," Paxton panted.

"You feel good," Sawyer said. "You taste good." He dipped his head and thrust his tongue into her mouth, sweeping around for a quick taste. "And your body looks amazing." He trailed his lips along her collarbone and then down her chest, pressing wet kisses to the shallow valley between her breasts. He pleasured her with his mouth, rolling his tongue around her taut peaked nipple, tugging it inside and sucking hard.

She squeezed her muscles, and Sawyer lost it. Clutching her ass, he pulled her to him and slammed into her body, over and over and over, his uncontrollable desire overriding everything else.

He felt Paxton explode as she cried out; the feel of her climaxing around him sent him over the edge. With one final thrust, he came, his body jerking, his entire being shuddering in an ecstasy that was so intoxicating Sawyer never wanted it to end.

Paxton burrowed herself more securely against Sawyer's naked chest, seeking his warmth now that the chill from outside was starting to seep in.

"You may want to check the settings on your central air unit," she told him. "I don't think you adjusted for tonight's cold front. It's freezing in here."

"You cold?" Sawyer wrapped his arm around her middle. "I have a better way of heating you up," he said as he buried his face against her neck.

Paxton squirmed, pretending she was trying to get away, when in reality she wasn't trying to do anything of the sort. She'd never felt more content than she did lying there wrapped in Sawyer's arms. It was as if he couldn't get enough of touching her. His fingers teased her bare shoulders, the nape of her neck, her collarbone. It was the closest she'd ever come to experiencing pure bliss.

They remained that way for long moments, resting comfortably together on the chaise underneath the cashmere throw Sawyer had taken from a hallway linen closet. But then Sawyer's voice broke into the silence.

"You have to tell me why, Pax," he said softly.

She knew this was coming, but she was no more ready to explain than she was ready to leave his arms.

But Paxton knew she owed him an explanation. Deciding to finally own up to what she'd done, she twisted around in his arms and faced him.

"Why did you leave the way you did?" Sawyer asked.

"It's simple," she said. "I felt guilty."

His head reared back. "That's definitely not what I was expecting. Why in the world would you have felt guilty?" His body stiffened. "Were you dating someone at the time? Did you use me to cheat on your boyfriend?"

"No." She shook her head. "I didn't have a boyfriend. But I did use you," she continued. Sawyer's eyes were filled with confusion. Paxton placed her hand on his chest. "That night, when you came into the bar, I could tell how much you were hurting. I wanted to help alleviate some of that pain."

"Which you most certainly did," he said.

"Except once we left the bar, your hurt and pain became second to me living out my fantasy. I've wanted you for so long, Sawyer, and all I could think about was finally having you for myself. I capitalized on your suffering. I knew you were drunk and vulnerable, and I used it to my advantage to get what I wanted."

Paxton braced herself for the backlash. Instead, she felt his chest start to rumble seconds before a roaring laugh poured forth from his mouth. She peered up at him.

"What's so funny?"

"You," Sawyer said. "You are so funny and so incredibly sweet. But you're clueless as hell, Pax. At least when it comes to this."

He trailed his fingers along her jawline in a gentle caress. "Is that really the reason you left?" he asked. "Because you felt guilty for using me?"

"Think about it, Sawyer. What if our roles were reversed, and you'd slept with me while I was hurting over my sick mother?"

"Pax, you didn't take advantage of me that night," he

said. "You gave me exactly what I needed, and I don't just mean sex with the girl who'd starred in every one of my teenage wet dreams. You gave me a chance to escape the realities of that day. I went to Harlon's hoping to drink away my troubles. But the alcohol didn't do anything compared to what you did for me."

He tenderly brushed his hand across her cheek. "Never feel guilty for that night, Paxton. That night ranks up there as one of the best nights of my life." He nudged behind her ear. "In case you were wondering, tonight is running a close second."

She smiled up at him, her heart nearly bursting with gratitude over the way he'd so selflessly assuaged the guilt she'd carried these past three years.

"You know," Sawyer began. "There is something you can do to send this night right to the top of the best night ever list."

Paxton couldn't contain her laugh as he suggestively waggled his brows. She wrapped her arms around his neck, pulled his head down and kissed him with everything she had.

Chapter 9

As she poured cranberry juice into a second short tumbler of vodka and ice, Paxton tried to fight the smile gradually stretching across her face. She wasn't known as a smiler, so she knew her constant grinning already seemed conspicuous to the regulars at the bar. But to have this smile on her face while the LSU Tigers were down by three touchdowns in the first quarter?

Yes, she definitely stood out in this crowd of sorry faces.

She would just have to stand out, because this smile was not going away, not with the naughty montage of the past twenty-four hours playing in her head. She paused as an involuntary tremor cascaded through her body. She'd experienced those more times than she could count today.

Paxton set the vodka cranberries in front of Reed

Jackson and the woman he had brought in with him tonight. She was the third different woman in his past three visits to the bar.

"I hope you two are having a good time tonight," Paxton said. "Reed, I'm not sure how you keep all these—" Reed's eyes went wide "—drink orders in line," she finished.

She turned to his date. "Most of the folks here stick to beer, but Reed puts my bartending skills to the test. He loves to try different things. Don't you, Reed?"

Paxton winked at him and left him at the bar with his eyes still wide.

She was in much too good of a mood to ruin Reed's fun. Multiple orgasms tended to put her in a good mood. She should make a point of having them more often.

The bar patrons kept her busy, with everyone wanting to drink their sorrows away after the disappointing start to the game. Paxton figured she would have to call in some designated driver reinforcements to make sure everyone got home safely tonight.

Once the demand waned, she turned her attention to restocking the bar before the next wave of drink orders came crashing through. Paxton stooped down and grabbed hold of the cardboard box she'd brought in from her car earlier.

"Hey, hey, hey." Donovan came up alongside her just as she set it on the shelf a few inches below the bar. "This is what I'm here for, hot mama." He picked it up, his eyes eager. "Okay, where do you need it?"

Paxton nodded at the bar. "Exactly where I just had it. And if you call me hot mama again, I'm knocking you over the head with a bottle of gin." She pointed at him. "And do *not* wink."

"Next time you need to pick up a box, you call me."

And, yes, the little pain in her ass still winked at her. If he didn't do such a great job helping them out…

Belinda rapped her knuckles on the bar to get their attention. "Donovan, Jessie needs more chicken wings. Can you get a case from the freezer outside?"

He nodded to Belinda, then looked back to Paxton. "Where's my thank-you kiss for helping with the box?"

"I'm instituting a sexual harassment policy," she said.

He grinned. "You know I love it when a woman plays hard to get, right?"

Paxton pointed at the kitchen door. "Go!"

Despite the dismal start to the game, the kitchen was hopping with orders for hot wings, loaded potato skins and fried pickles. Maybe the crowd was eating their feelings as well as drowning their sorrows in liquor.

LSU began the second quarter with a quick touch-down followed by a fumble recovery in Alabama territory, and the mood around the bar instantly perked up. Of course, that meant more drinks were bought, this time to celebrate. She would definitely need to recruit more designated drivers.

When an electrified tingle drizzled down her spine, Paxton didn't even have to look toward the entrance to know who had just arrived. She looked, anyway. The drizzle turned into a torrential downpour of lust as she spotted Sawyer striding toward her with a smile so sexy it did things to her insides that should be illegal.

He wedged himself between two occupied bar stools and leaned onto the bar.

"Hello," he greeted her, his voice low and sensual and infused with just enough barely veiled hunger to make Paxton's body go liquid.

"Hello," she returned. "Can I get you a drink?"

"What tastes good around here?" His eyes dropped to her waist. "Besides…you know."

Her entire body went up in flames.

"Stop that," she mouthed.

"No," he mouthed back, slowly shaking his head.

Paxton leaned over the bar and put her lips to his ear. "Just because you saw me naked for the second time doesn't mean you get to talk to me any way you want."

"Technically, it was the third time. You were foolish enough to put a shirt on for a while, remember?"

Yes, she remembered that lapse in judgment. She put on his T-shirt to go to the kitchen for a glass of soda. He immediately stripped it from her body when she returned to his room and made love to her for the second time last night. They'd fallen asleep naked in each other's arms, awakening with the sun and making love again this morning.

And then again in the shower.

Despite it being a Saturday morning, they'd gone to the law office to get a few hours of work done in preparation for Monday's town hall meeting. The concentration it took to actually work once they got there was, by far, the greatest feat Paxton had achieved this year. Somehow they managed to get most of the agenda for the town hall meeting nailed down between a barrage of stolen kisses and one shoulder rub that got wildly out of hand. A shudder ran through her body at the memory.

Activity at the bar picked up at halftime, so Paxton left Sawyer to his beer as she filled drink orders at lightning speed. Once the game started again and patrons turned their attention back to the televisions, she called for Belinda to take over bartending duties so she could have a breather.

She walked around the bar to Sawyer, who hadn't so much as turned his head to look at the game the entire time he'd been sitting there. Despite being Mr. Football, he made it more than clear with his actions that he was there to see *her*. The realization sent a heady sensation through her body.

"Can I tear you away from your bar stool?" she asked.

"You can tear me away from anything you please. You have my undivided attention."

His words should have made her feel empowered, but Paxton realized he held the same power over her. She couldn't think of anything he could ask her to do right now that she wouldn't gladly oblige. The most astonishing thing in all of this was the fact that those thoughts didn't scare her senseless. She, who prided herself on always being in control, on being independent. She would willingly do whatever Sawyer asked of her.

As she took him by the hand, she noticed Belinda looking at them as if she wanted to snatch Paxton away from him and put her protectively behind her back. Paxton looked at her with a raised brow, but her mother didn't respond. She just continued to look at them in that strange, overly cautious way.

Paxton guided Sawyer into the kitchen, where she picked up the load of scraps Jessie had placed on a tin dish for Heinz; then she led him out of the back door to the outside storage shed, which held a second deep freezer and the cleaning supplies.

Using a metal rod tied to the door handle, Paxton rapped on the edge of the tin dish a couple of times, calling for Heinz. The oversize mutt crawled from his favorite spot underneath the bar and galloped over to them, his ears and jowls flopping.

"Here you go, boy," Paxton said, setting his food before him. She grabbed his empty water dish and filled it using the tap that ran from the bar.

"Does your mom know you missed the dog more than you missed her while you were in Little Rock?"

Paxton gave him the evil eye. "You'd better not say anything."

Sawyer's shoulders shook with his laugh. "I may just have to use that for blackmail."

She tried to maintain her harsh look but couldn't hold it together.

"To be honest, Belinda probably already knows. Heinz has had my heart since I found him hurt on the side of Highway 421 about eight years ago. He was still a puppy."

"Why that name? It sounds like he was named after a banker or something."

"Actually, he's named after the steak sauce."

Sawyer's forehead wrinkled in confusion.

"Heinz 57?" Paxton said. "As in fifty-seven varieties? He's made up of so many different breeds that we can't decide exactly what he is. He's a mutt in the truest sense, but I love him."

"I'd say the feeling is mutual," Sawyer said, gesturing to the way the dog schmoozed against her leg now that he was done with his dinner. "Of course, if you fed me Jessie's cooking and rubbed me behind the ear, I'd do the same thing. Maybe we should try that later."

A wicked gleam shining in his eyes, Sawyer took a step toward her. He stopped when Heinz let out a low menacing growl.

"Heel, boy," Paxton called over her shoulder. She wrapped her arms around Sawyer's neck and backed him up against the side of the shed.

"I know this is asking for trouble," she said as she kissed just below his jawline. The faint stubble from his five o'clock shadow caused all kinds of sensations to swirl throughout her bloodstream. "But I can't seem to help it."

"Don't you even try," Sawyer said, reversing their positions and pinning her against the building. As his mouth zeroed in on her lips, his hands went straight for her ass, clutching it tightly in his palms.

A moan crawled from Paxton's throat as she undulated against the part of him swelling against her stomach.

"This is crazy. This is crazy. This is crazy," she murmured over and over against his lips.

"This is right," Sawyer returned. "But if we don't stop, your mom will probably find us together and beat me away with a frying pan."

Paxton chuckled at the image, but it also roused her curiosity. "I'm not sure why she's so hostile toward you," Paxton said. "Belinda is never like that."

He shrugged, his lips seeking out her neck. "She probably knows what we did last night and doesn't want me corrupting you."

"It's a bit too late for that," Paxton said with a laugh.

"As much as I love feeling up her daughter, I don't want to feel her wrath." He nudged along her collarbone, moistening the skin with his wet kisses. "I know it's a drive, but do you want to come over to my place once the game is over? Please, don't say anything but yes."

"Yes," Paxton said, loving the desperation in his voice. It matched what she was feeling.

Goodness, why did she fight this for so long?

"I'll see if Donovan can take over for me behind the bar. Then I'll follow you in my car."

"You know," he said, pulling her closer and trailing his tongue along the seam of her lips. "You could just pack up enough clothes for the week. You wouldn't have to worry about that long commute. Hell, we could decide not to go into the office at all. Just work naked in bed all day."

The thought of that set Paxton's body on fire, but she knew she couldn't. Spending the night was one thing. Spending the week was something she would need more time to process before she agreed to do it.

"I doubt any work would get done," she said. "Maybe we should leave the naked fun to the weekend."

Sawyer growled his disapproval, then pulled her bottom lip between his teeth, biting gently before taking her lips in another long, decadent kiss that had her body humming with need.

The unmistakable squeak of the bar's back screen door put an end to their sexy party.

"Pax?" Belinda called.

Paxton and Sawyer broke apart like a couple of teenagers who had been caught necking. A flutter of excitement lifted her belly. She'd never had the experience of being caught with a boy back in high school.

"Paxton?" Belinda said, walking over to them.

"I was just on my way," she said. She and Sawyer were both grinning at each other. "I'll see you in a little while," she said.

He gave her another kiss, waved goodbye to her mom and headed for the parking lot.

"How serious is this thing with Sawyer Robertson?" Belinda asked. "What's really going on between you two?"

Paxton looked at her with a raised brow. "You sure you want to know? We share a lot, but I'm not sure you want to hear about the really good sex I'm having. I usually save that kind of talk for Shayla."

The sight of her mother's stern jaw made her feel as if she were a teenager again.

"I told you already that you don't have to worry about me," Paxton said, pulling her mother in for a hug. "It's adorable that you still do, but really, Mom, I can take care of myself."

Belinda frowned. "It sounds strange to hear you call me Mom," she said. "Stick with Belinda. That I'm used to." Her face became serious again. "Be careful, Pax. I don't want you getting hurt."

"Sawyer won't hurt me." Paxton shook her head. "My heart is well guarded. You taught me how to do that."

"Well at least I was good for something," her mother said.

"If I had to list all the things you're good for, we'd be here until next week. Now, let's get back to work, so I can get out of here," Paxton said, wrapping an arm around her shoulder and heading for the bar. She bumped Belinda with her hip. "I've got good sex waiting for me at the end of my shift."

Her mother slapped her on the arm. "Stop trying to make me jealous."

Paxton pulled into the parking lot of the high school auditorium, the only place in town that was big enough to hold tonight's town hall meeting. Her mouth fell open at the sight of all the cars already crowding the parking lot.

"And here I thought I was early for once," she muttered.

She knew there would be some interest, but she never imagined a meeting about the mundane technical details of a flood protection system would suddenly be the hottest ticket in town.

She spotted Sawyer standing in front of his open trunk. He waved her over and pointed to a spot two places down. By the time she reached his car, he had an armful of topography maps.

"Hey there," he said, closing the car's trunk with his elbow.

"Thanks for saving me a spot," Paxton said. She reached over to help alleviate some of his burden, but he moved the maps out of her reach.

"I've got this." He looked over both shoulders, then gave her a swift but deep kiss. "But this is what I need."

Paxton's brow peaked. "Stealing kisses in the school parking lot?"

The devilish grin that slipped across his lips held so many naughty promises. "Don't you remember I played baseball, too? Stealing bases was my specialty. But I much prefer stealing kisses, especially when it comes to yours."

Paxton leaned over and whispered in his ear, "For future reference, you don't have to steal them." Then, despite his protest, she slipped several of the cylindrical cartons from his hold and started for the brick building.

"It looks like this is the place to be tonight," Paxton called over her shoulder.

"Interest is high," Sawyer said. "News broke about the potential change in the flood zones. Everyone is concerned about what it may mean for insurance rates."

Paxton's footsteps halted. She slowly turned to face him. "How did that get out?"

Sawyer shrugged. "Small town. Someone may have heard us talking about it at the Jazzy Bean."

"Are people upset or just curious?"

"Both," Sawyer said.

She pitched her head back and groaned. "I do not need this."

"It doesn't matter what you're doing, Pax. You'll always have at least a few community members who will have a bone to pick with you."

"Sure, but I'm used to folks being upset over the inconvenience caused by the construction. You know, roads being closed around the site and things like that. I'm not used to dealing with hostility this early into a project."

"This is Gauthier. You don't have to worry about the crowd turning hostile on you, but you are talking about people's money," Sawyer said. "They're going to be concerned."

"Wait? Is Sawyer Robertson actually lecturing *me* about money?"

"Don't, Paxton," he said in a warning tone.

"I do believe *I* was the one who told *you* that people were not going to take too kindly to having to pay more in insurance, especially when so many of them were screwed by the insurance companies during the last flood."

"We both knew this would be an issue, just as we both

know the new flood maps are necessary." Sawyer looked her squarely in the eyes. "We've been over this, Pax."

"I know." She blew out an irritated sigh. "Don't worry—I'm not going to stray from the plan."

They were in this together. They'd devised a strategy for dealing with questions regarding the elevation maps.

Whether or not they were getting the new flood maps was no longer the question; everyone—from the powers that be at Bolt-Myer to Sawyer's superiors at the Army Corp of Engineers—agreed that this project could not go forward without the new maps. Their task tonight was to explain to the people of Gauthier just why they were needed and convince them that it was in the best interest of the town.

Yeah, she was not looking forward to this.

Paxton held the door open for Sawyer and followed him into the auditorium. If she was to give a rough estimate, she'd say there were at least a hundred people already filling the seats. The atmosphere suffusing the room held a tenseness that made the hair on the back of Paxton's neck stand on end.

She spotted Shayla, who was at a table that had been set up in the corner. Six carry-away cardboard cartons bearing the Jazzy Bean's logo sat atop the table, along with a stack of paper coffee cups, cream, sugar packets and other coffee fixings.

"Thanks for bringing this," Paxton said, giving her a hug as she greeted her.

Shayla hugged her back, then punched her in the arm.

"Hey!" Paxton said, rubbing the spot where she'd taken the hit. "What was that for?"

Shayla leaned in and whispered fiercely, "I didn't get a postorgasm call."

"Do you ever call me postorgasm?" Paxton asked. Then she held up a hand. "Don't answer that."

"Did you two do it or not?" Shayla asked.

Paxton glanced over her shoulder. "Yes," she finally said. Shayla started to squeal, but Paxton seared her with a look that said she'd better shut it up right now. She spotted Sawyer coming up to them. "I'll tell you about it later."

"Hey, is Matt Gauthier here yet?" Sawyer asked. He looked at Shayla, whose smile was so wide Paxton didn't know how her face didn't split in half. Then he looked at her, one brow raised, his eyes lit with amusement.

"Don't worry," Shayla said. "She didn't kiss and tell. Yet. And, no, Matt isn't here, but the meeting doesn't start for another twenty minutes. He'll be here on time. He always is."

"It's okay if he's running a little late," Paxton said. "Mya is before him on the agenda, anyway. I've asked her to take the reins when it comes to running the meeting. Residents have come to trust Mya. She'll put people at ease."

Shayla went back to smiling, and Paxton went back to wanting to knock her upside the head.

As the room continued to fill, so did the anxiety cluttering Paxton's chest. She didn't want to think about how it would be received if they told the residents that they may have to spend several hundred dollars more a year in flood insurance. And that was on the low end. Some people—those in the most vulnerable areas, which were also some of the poorest areas—may have to pay upward of a thousand extra dollars a year if the revamped flood zones raised their levels too much.

Paxton didn't have to try to put herself in their shoes.

She'd worn their shoes for years. Her mother still did. They both knew exactly how it felt to pinch every penny you could find until old Abe Lincoln squealed. She wouldn't be surprised if most of the people in her part of town didn't even have flood insurance. They were probably relying on prayer to keep their homes and possessions safe. Paxton couldn't help but feel like a traitor for going along with this plan that may put those who could afford insurance under even more financial duress.

But the science didn't lie. They were doing what needed to be done in order to build a flood protection system that would hopefully prevent them from ever having to cash in on those insurance policies. Still, she was certain some of the people filling these seats wouldn't see things the same way.

By the time the meeting got under way it seemed as if half the town had shown up.

Mya Dubois-Anderson took the floor and, in her composed yet authoritative way, went over the meeting agenda, stressing several times throughout her initial spiel that questions would be taken at the end of the presentation.

By the time Mya called her to take center stage, Paxton had calmed the nervous energy running through her enough to stop her hands from shaking. Public speaking had never been her strong suit, but she had given this type of pitch enough over her career that she could recite it in her sleep.

But things were different this time. This time it was personal.

Paxton couldn't look out over the crowd of familiar faces—some skeptical, others hopeful, some completely expressionless—and ignore how deeply personal this all felt. These people trusted her. Even the skeptics wanted to believe that she had their best interests at heart. She didn't want to let them down.

She gave the crowd a brief overview of what they were planning to do and what they could expect in the upcoming months once the actual construction commenced. The crowd gave her their undivided attention, and then gave the same to Matt Gauthier, who had come in a few minutes later. Sawyer closed out the presentation with his explanation of the mechanics of the flood protection system. Paxton was impressed with the way he explained it all in layman's terms, without coming across as if he were patronizing anyone. Some of the engineers she worked with at Bolt-Myer could learn a thing or two from him.

"The citizens of Gauthier should also be applauded for approving the millage tax that will be used to fund the rest of the project along with the upkeep," Sawyer said. "This is going to be a long effort, but after what many of you experienced with Tropical Storm Lucy, I'm sure we all understand just why it's so important."

He glanced at Paxton before turning back to the audience. "If you all could bear with me, I'm going to go off script for just a minute."

Paxton tried to curb the quick shot of anxiety that slashed through her. Going off script was never a good thing in her book.

"Paxton and I, along with several people from the state, have visited the properties that received the most damage," Sawyer started. "But I think it's only fair that we give everyone whose lives were negatively affected the opportunity to voice your grievances. We want to hear your stories. We want to know how this has affected you both financially and emotionally these past months."

Only moments ago Paxton had wanted to strangle him, but if she didn't think it would cause a firestorm of gossip around town, she would kiss Sawyer right now.

This was what the people in this town needed to hear—that someone cared about the struggles they had endured. It wasn't just the houses that took in several feet that made this flood protection system necessary. Even one inch of standing water could cost a home owner thousands of dollars in flooring repair.

And that was exactly the kind of stories they heard as, one by one, citizens shared how their lives had changed in the aftermath of Tropical Storm Lucy. Hearing about the damage was bad enough, but Paxton heard so many tales of insurance companies not covering repairs that she thought she would be sick.

Just when she thought they would get out of this meeting unscathed, Clifford Mayes, the town's retired policeman, posed a question that sent a ripple of tension through the crowd.

"What about these flood maps you want to draw up?" Mr. Mayes asked in his gravelly voice. "I heard they would make our insurance rates spike."

"That's what I heard, too," Nathan Robottom said. "The insurance we already have didn't want to cover the storm damage. Paying more is just throwing good money after bad."

The number of people nodding as others aired their grievances about the potential insurance rate hikes continued to increase.

Paxton's head instantly started to pound, but she couldn't refute a single claim because they were right.

There was a better than average chance that the same people who were screwed by the insurance companies after Tropical Storm Lucy would be screwed again if another storm hit.

She glanced over at Sawyer. The worry clouding his face told her exactly what he was feeling on the inside. This was as hard for him to hear as it was for her. Sawyer was a fixer. He was the kind of man who wanted to come in on his white horse and save the day.

But even the powerful Robertson name and money could not save everyone in town from financial ruin following a storm.

"I'm not as concerned about the insurance rates as I am about our property values," Jamal Johnson said.

Jamal had moved from Arizona to Gauthier several years ago. An architect, he and Phylicia Phillips had renovated her family's beautiful Victorian home, turning it into the town's only bed-and-breakfast. Belle Maison was in an area that wasn't classified as a flood zone, but Paxton couldn't be sure what category it would fall into once the new maps were drawn.

"This can be even more costly than just paying a higher insurance premium," Jamal said. "If your property is in a part of town that is designated as a flood zone, the property values will plummet."

"And developers will come in and start scooping up the land that isn't in flood zones," Mr. Mayes added. "That's what happened in Maplesville. You'd better believe it'll happen here, too."

As the residents continued making the case against the new flood maps, Paxton couldn't help but be moved by their plight. Tonight had changed her outlook on her career. She would never walk into a town hall meeting again and address a crowd of citizens with the detachment she once felt. Before, she was just doing her job. But her job was not all about budgets and engineering specs and beating her coworker, Clay Ridgley, to the finish line.

This was about people's lives. This was about years of hard work and sacrifice, about people who had given everything to make life better for their families. She had to look no further than her own mother to see the face of that hard work and sacrifice.

The weight of what they were doing hit Paxton with enough force to steal the breath from her lungs. The decisions she and Sawyer made in that conference room would have a lasting effect on the people in this town for generations to come.

This was *her* hometown. These were *her* people.

Paxton knew she would never be able to look at herself in the mirror if she didn't do right by them. She just needed to make sure what they were doing really was the best thing for Gauthier.

Sawyer rested his head on the rim of the sofa while running his fingers through Paxton's short locks. They had been in this position for the past hour, her head on his lap, face turned to the television. Neither of them paid much attention to the crime drama on the screen.

He'd tried to cajole her into driving out to Maplesville for a late dinner after this evening's town hall meeting, but she had declined, saying she just wasn't up to it. Honestly, neither was he. Instead, Sawyer had made them both peanut butter and jelly sandwiches, which they'd eaten while standing at his kitchen island.

He'd given up trying to read her mood. The only

thing he was sure about was that it had changed drastically in the twenty-four hours since they'd last been here. When they'd sat in this same spot last night, they'd both been naked, and the atmosphere had been a heck of a lot more fun.

Another twenty minutes of him gently stroking her hair passed before Paxton stirred and asked, "Why did you sell your parents' home?"

Sawyer's fingers paused midstroke. "Where did that come from?"

"Even though I've been here nearly every night for the past week, this is the first chance I've had to really look at your home."

Sawyer dipped his head and placed a sweet kiss on her ear before whispering, "That's because I've kept you too busy with other things to worry about giving you a tour of the house."

Her sexy laugh triggered a hardening in his groin.

"This place is nice, but I can imagine that your old house was even more spectacular." She turned in his lap, resting the back of her head on his thighs so she could look up at him. "Why did you sell your childhood home so quickly? Was it because you had no intentions of returning to Gauthier after you got married?"

Sawyer thought about that for a moment before he shook his head. "No, I knew I would be back," he answered. "Even though I still have my condo in New Orleans, I always planned to return to Gauthier. I just didn't want to live in that house."

"Too many bad memories? I mean, with you losing both of your parents there, I can only imagine."

"Actually, it's a bit more practical than that. I just don't need that much space. Funny thing is, I found out that my mom and dad both thought the house was too big for our family, too."

"Wait. So neither of your parents wanted that big house?"

"Nope." He went back to stroking her head.

"So…why?"

"My mom and dad both grew up poor. When they were first married, Dad promised to build her a house fit for a queen. Once he became successful, he did. She thought it was too big, but she didn't tell him because she didn't want to hurt his feelings. He didn't say anything for the same reason."

Paxton burst out laughing. "I'm sorry," she said. "But that's so incredibly sweet."

"They were embarrassingly sweet," he said. "They would have been just fine living in this house," he said, gesturing to his living room, which was still fairly large by most standards but was nothing compared with the mansion he'd grown up in.

"I was so jealous of your childhood home," Paxton admitted in a soft voice.

"Hey, Matt Gauthier's family had a bigger house than mine."

"Yeah, but he's a Gauthier. They're royalty around here." She looked up at him. "And I didn't have a crush on Matt."

Sawyer couldn't believe the pleasure he derived from her sweetly whispered admission. Yet it killed him to think about how much time they'd wasted.

"You do realize how ridiculous it is that we both had a thing for each other yet were too cowardly to say anything for all this time, right?"

"I doubt I would have been able to handle all of this before now," she said. "It still doesn't feel real."

"What doesn't feel real?"

"This," she said. "Being here with you, having you stroke my hair, lying here as if I belong in your arms."

"This is exactly where you belong, Pax."

She smiled up at him, but it was too conciliatory to convince Sawyer that she actually believed him.

"I wish I'd had the chance to see your old house before you sold it. I used to covet that place."

"I'm sure the new owners would let me take you for a tour," Sawyer said.

She chuckled and shook her head. "It wouldn't be the same. One of the reasons I loved it is because you were there." Her statement caused a pang of sweet joy to pierce his chest. "You know, I never told this to Shayla, but I used to envy her so much back in high school because she used to go to your house all the time."

"Shayla and I were just friends. There was never anything between us."

"Oh, I know. Believe me, she would have told me if there was. But just the fact that she was your friend was enough to make me envy her. That she hung out with you at Jessie's after the game and rode around in your truck."

"I was never brave enough to ask you to do any of those things," Sawyer admitted. "I thought you would have turned me down."

"I would have," she said. "Back then, there was nothing you could have said to me that would have convinced me that I belonged in your world."

Sawyer brushed his fingers along her jaw before using them to turn her face toward him.

"Why does it seem as if you still don't believe you belong in my world, Paxton?"

"Because it still doesn't feel real," she repeated.

"What is it going to take to make you see that this has always been real?"

Sawyer moved back slightly as she pushed herself up and into a sitting position. She tucked one leg underneath her, then reached over and squeezed his thigh. "This has been fun, but let's not kid ourselves, Sawyer. We're just too—"

"Don't say 'different,'" Sawyer warned.

"Telling me not to say it doesn't make it any less true," she said.

Sawyer shut his eyes and tipped his head back on the edge of the sofa. He kneaded the bridge of his nose and released a sigh. What else could he do to make this woman see that they belonged together?

"I know you don't like to hear it," Paxton said, "but you don't have to look any further than tonight's meeting to see just how different we are. I recognized the fear in those faces I saw tonight, Sawyer. That anxiety they're feeling over the potential insurance rate hike? I've felt that."

"We've been over this already, Paxton. Those new maps are necessary."

"Are they really?"

"Are you seriously questioning this again?" Sawyer asked.

"What if what happened with Tropical Storm Lucy was just a freak occurrence?"

"This is the Gulf South, Paxton. It's hurricane prone."

"But how many major hurricanes does this area get? There hasn't been a catastrophic storm since Hurricane

Katrina, and Gauthier didn't suffer nearly as much from that storm as other areas. What if these new elevation maps cause everyone's insurance to spike, but there are no storms for another twenty years? We could cause people to go into financial ruin just as surely as a storm would."

"I won't allow anyone to go into financial ruin over this," he said.

"How can you prevent it? The Cheryl Ann Robertson Foundation cannot supplement the entire town's flood insurance."

He shrugged. "Maybe it can."

"Sawyer," she said in a warning tone. "You cannot bail out all of Gauthier."

"I won't have to," he said. "Just trust me on this, Paxton. We're doing the right thing."

She looked doubtful, but, thank goodness, she didn't argue the point any further. Instead she moved over to his side of the sofa again, curling up on his lap. Sawyer ran his palm along her body, stopping at her backside and giving it a firm squeeze.

"Do you want me to finally take you on a tour of the house?" he asked.

A naughty grin played on her lips as she looked up at him. "Only if the final stop is your bedroom."

Chapter 10

Balancing a cardboard cup-holder tray in one hand while holding a bag of pastries underneath his chin, Sawyer opened the conference room door and stepped inside.

"Shayla was out of those cranberry oatmeal bars you like, so I got you—" He stopped midsentence at the intense look clouding Paxton's face.

He set the coffee and pastries on the table and walked over to her desk. She held up her index finger, the universal I'll-get-to-you-in-a-minute gesture.

He perched on the edge of the table and folded his arms across his chest, not even bothering to go back to the CAD drawing he'd been working on before he went to the Jazzy Bean to get them both an afternoon snack.

With only her "ums" and "okays" to go on, it was difficult to glean exactly what was being discussed. But

Sawyer didn't have to hear both sides to know that whatever it was, it was significant. If it had anything to do with her mother or her dog, Paxton would have left the office without a second thought; he could only conclude that the call was related to the job.

He fought the urge to go directly to the worst-case scenario, but Sawyer had worked on enough state-funded projects to know how swiftly they could move from all systems go to worst-case scenario. The funding could get pulled in a minute. All it would take was someone at the executive level deeming another project more important. Gauthier's flood protection would be put on hold, funds would be diverted and he would be reassigned to another project before the week was out.

And Paxton would be on her way back to Little Rock.

It wasn't a question as to which made him more nauseous. As important as it was to this entire region that a capable flood protection system be in place, the thought of Paxton leaving made him physically ache.

It didn't matter that she would be only six hours away and that he could go up there every single weekend if he chose to—which Sawyer had already decided he would do once she returned. He was supposed to have at least another week with her. He was counting on that week before they had to figure out the "what's next" part of their relationship.

An acute sense of desperation swept through him.

He still was uncertain whether or not she even considered them to be in an actual relationship. Maybe she really *was* just living out her fantasy of having a bit of fun with her high school crush, and once this project was done, they would be done, too.

But Sawyer refused to accept that. She'd run away

from him once before, and instead of going after her, he'd married someone he didn't love and wasted three years that could have been spent building a life with Paxton.

Dammit, he was *ready* to build a life with her.

He studied her profile as she listened to whoever was speaking on the other end of the line. Those delicate cheekbones were pronounced as her lips tightened with increased tension. Even with the smooth skin of her brow furrowing, she was still so damn beautiful that she took his breath away.

When she finally ended the call a couple of minutes later, Sawyer braced himself for the news. It would determine how much time he had with her before she packed up her things and headed back to Arkansas.

"That was John, my supervisor at Bolt-Myer," Paxton said.

"I assumed as much. Are they pulling this project?"

She shook her head. "No, no, nothing like that. There's a second team from Bolt-Myer touring a flood protection system that's closer to one of the possible alternatives being considered for Gauthier. Instead of driving out to Mobile to tour that barrier system, he wants us to join them."

"Is that it?" Sawyer's relief was so swift that his shoulders physically dropped.

"We have to leave tomorrow, so I'll need to change our travel arrangements." She swirled her chair around to face him. "But there's still a problem," she said.

That feeling of lead filled his stomach again as he took in the seriousness of her expression. "Bolt-Myer is concerned about the timetable. Of course, John wouldn't come right out and say it because he approved the survey team, but he's very skilled at giving not-so-subtle hints when he has an issue."

"The surveyors are done," Sawyer said. "We have a special team at the Army Corps working around the clock to get the new maps drawn up. Does he realize how tough it is to get any state agency to work overtime on something that isn't critical?"

"Yes, he knows," she said. "John is just being John. That's just the way he is."

"Well, you can tell John that he's an idiot."

"He's my boss," Paxton pointed out. "He holds my career in his hands. I generally try to refrain from calling him an idiot, as hard as that can be sometimes."

She blew out a sigh before continuing. "Anyway, I told him the maps will be done within the next couple of days, which mollified him a bit, but the timetable is just one of the issues he has with this project. He was much more concerned with what he's calling 'dwindling community confidence.'"

Sawyer furrowed his forehead. "What makes him think the community doesn't have confidence in what we're doing?"

"Apparently, there's video on both YouTube and Instagram of the town hall meeting from the other night. He's concerned with how heated things became."

Sawyer pointed in the general direction of the school where the meeting had been held. "He called *that* heated? I've seen more heated arguments over a bad call by the refs during a football game. That wasn't people being upset with you or Bolt-Myer—they're upset about the situation in general. People in Gauthier are passionate. They need to understand that."

"You know that, and I know that," Paxton said. "But

the powers that be at Bolt-Myer get edgy when community members show dissatisfaction."

"It cannot be that drastic, Pax."

"Goodness, Sawyer, why can't you understand this?" She threw her hands in the air. "I've explained it to you before. We may work in the same industry, but we're operating in two entirely different worlds. Do you know how many engineering firms we're up against every time we bid on a project? One viral video of a disgruntled community member going off at a town hall meeting can lead to Bolt-Myer never working on another project in Louisiana again. There are too many other capable firms the state can turn to.

"Bolt-Myer can't write off Nathan Robottom's rant the other night as just a community member mouthing off because it could mean the difference between tens of millions of dollars in state contracts. I can't just write off John's concerns because it could mean the difference between me moving into a project director or even a division head role, or being stuck as a project manager for the rest of my career. It really is that drastic."

She brought one hand up to her temple and rubbed. "I'm sorry," she said. "It's just that I have a lot riding on this, Sawyer. Every single project I work on can make or break my career. The pressure is enough to suffocate me sometimes, but it's been that way my entire life. It has never, ever been easy for me, but I do what I have to do, and I get the job done."

He sat back for a moment, unable to even come up with a response after her impassioned speech.

She was right. As much as it pained him to admit it, every single thing she had said was right. He'd faced his share of hardships—he'd watched both his parents suffer through cancer and buried them both before he turned thirty-five—but he had never had to endure the kind of pressure Paxton faced every single day. And she managed it with far more strength and grace than he could ever muster.

It made him love her even more.

"I'm sorry," she said again, shaking her head. "I didn't mean to go off on you like that."

"It's okay," Sawyer said. "I needed to hear it." He walked over to her desk and captured her hands, bringing them to his lips. "You tried to tell me before, but it wasn't until just now that I realized how much harder it has been for you."

"Don't turn me into some martyr," she said.

"I'm not. I'm pointing out how strong you are. And you're right—we need to do whatever we can to make sure this project comes in on budget and on time. It's your career on the line here." He clamped his hands together. "So, what do we have to do to make Idiot John happy?"

"You up for that road trip?" she asked.

"I'll gas up the car."

"Actually, I need to book us some flights."

"We're flying?"

"Yeah," Paxton said, turning around to face her computer. "You may be familiar with the site they're touring. It's in southern Illinois." Sawyer's stomach tanked, already sensing what she was about to say. "Just outside of another small town called Cairo."

Paxton struggled to maintain her calm as she sat across from Sawyer at the hotel restaurant where they had met the engineering team from Bolt-Myer. If she had known Clay Ridgely would be here, she would have made up an excuse for both she and Sawyer to forgo this trip. She was certain after her coworker's third thinly veiled sexist joke of the night that Sawyer was going to reach across the table and choke him. Thankfully, the social aspect of the evening was over and talk had moved to business.

Or maybe things were about to get worse.

"I heard you hit a couple of snags on your project, Paxton," Clay said as he sipped the whiskey that was against company regulations to indulge in on a business trip. Not as if that mattered to Clay.

"I wouldn't call it a snag," she said. "We're simply being thorough. It would be foolish and irresponsible to install a flood protection system that could possibly fail to protect some areas."

"You're going to be over budget, aren't you?" Clay asked, his smile sly.

"Anyone with any sense would recognize that coming in slightly over budget is nothing compared to the toll it would take on a community if it floods," Sawyer said in a tone so thick with disgust that only an idiot wouldn't realize just how pissed he was.

Of course, Clay *was* an idiot, so the icy atmosphere around the table was lost on him.

"Maybe in your line of work," Clay said with a guffaw. "But that's not how we do things in the private sector, buddy."

"Well, maybe the private sector should change its practices," Sawyer said.

"Spoken like a state engineer," Clay said, clapping his hand on Sawyer's shoulder.

It was obvious that her coworker had no idea Sawyer

was ready to pummel him. For just a second, Paxton was tempted to let them go at it, but she knew it would only cause more problems. She quickly turned the conversation to a fellow coworker who had just won a bid for a nuclear power plant upgrade, the first for Bolt-Myer.

She was so relieved when the bill finally arrived that she nearly cried. She wasn't sure she could stand another ten minutes of the tension around the table—a tension everyone other than Clay seemed to feel.

He took the bill and made a production of slipping his credit card in the folder, as if he were a big spender taking the crew out for dinner. Paxton knew he'd have his expense report filled out before he got on the plane tomorrow.

When they finally left the restaurant, she walked in step with Sawyer. She could tell by the set of his jaw that he was still fuming.

"Give me ten minutes," Paxton whispered. "I'll meet you in your room."

They'd booked separate rooms so as not to fuel any kind of rumors. Paxton went into her room and changed out of her favorite travel outfit, a dark brown skirt and matching jacket made of a forgivable fabric that was hard to wrinkle. She pulled on yoga pants and a roomy T-shirt, then waited another five minutes before grabbing her toiletry case and heading three doors down to Sawyer's room.

She got a text message from him just as she arrived at his door.

Where R U?

When he answered her knock, she held the phone up

to him. "Don't you think you're old enough to text like an adult? It's only four additional characters to actually spell out the words *are* and *you*."

"Would you get in here," Sawyer said, pulling her into the room.

The first thing he did was kiss her as if it had been twenty years since they'd last seen each other instead of twenty minutes. Once she was breathless and losing feeling in her legs, he finally let go of her lips, but he held on to the rest of her.

With his hands still clamped around her upper arms, he pulled away slightly and said, "That Clay guy is terrible."

"Like stepfather, like stepson," Paxton said. His brow furrowed. "Clay is my supervisor, John's stepson."

"Oh, you gotta be kidding me," Sawyer said.

"Yes. We call him Clay the Jackass in the office. Rather fitting, don't you think?"

"That's an insult to jackasses around the world." He took her by the hand and led her to bed, sitting up against the headboard and motioning for her to join him.

Paxton crawled onto the bed and into his lap, turning around and fitting herself against him. She pulled his arms around her, resting them just under her breasts, and leaned her head against his solid chest.

"Now do you see why I'm so determined to get the project in Gauthier done on time? Clay is my number one competition when the next project director position opens up. Don't be fooled by that passive-aggressive crap you saw at dinner tonight. He hates me, and the feeling is mutual."

"Why does he hate you?"

"Because I'm a better project manager, and John has

no choice but to give me my due. There's nothing he can do to dispute it."

"So, if you come in over budget and behind schedule on Gauthier's flood protection system, it's exactly the kind of thing he can use against you."

"Correct," Paxton said.

"Why didn't you say this from the very beginning?" She looked over her shoulder. "Maybe because I didn't want to look petty and spiteful?"

"Nothing wrong with pettiness and spite in my book, especially when it comes to showing up a jerk like that," Sawyer said. "We're going to get that revised draft of the ICP done on time, even if I don't get to sleep for a week."

A smile drew across her lips as she peered up at him. "You're willing to lose sleep for me?"

"Damn right," Sawyer said. "Of course, the reason we won't get any sleep tonight has nothing to do with your stupid coworker. In fact," he said as he caught the hem of her shirt and pulled it over her head. "When it comes to what we're about to do, I don't want thoughts of Clay the Jackass in your head at all."

She wrapped her arms around his neck. "I don't think that will be a problem."

She returned the favor of divesting him of his shirt before laying him flat on his back and having her way with him.

It was yet another fantasy fulfilled as she took control of their lovemaking, pinning Sawyer's hands on either side of his head and climbing on top of him. After getting rid of their pants and underwear, Paxton grabbed the condom he'd set on the bedside table, rolled it over his rock-solid erection and quickly guided him inside her.

Their twin moans of ecstasy rang throughout the

room as she lowered herself onto his lap, taking his full length inside and rocking slowly back and forth. Sawyer lifted up from the bed and caught her nipples in his mouth, first one, then the other. He licked and sucked while she pumped up and down; the rhythm of his mouth increased with every thrust of her hips. Paxton braced her hands over his solid abs, seeking purchase as she dived down and rose up, impaling herself on his hard flesh until she shattered in a swarm of sensation that radiated throughout her body.

An hour later, Paxton pulled Sawyer's arm across her body and tucked it underneath her side. The slow and steady beat of his heart against her back was the most soothing feeling she could imagine. The desire to feel this every day for the rest of her life was so strong it scared her. She ached to fall asleep each night with him right beside her, to wake up every morning wrapped in his arms. She wanted to share her life with him.

How had she allowed this to happen?

It was so cliché. The poor girl from the wrong side of Landreaux Creek falling for the richest boy in town. But she couldn't deny it. She'd fallen for him in every possible way.

"You're thinking really hard," Sawyer whispered against her ear.

She looked up over her shoulder. "How do you know that?"

"Because you aren't talking."

"So if I'm not talking, that means I'm thinking too hard?"

He flipped her onto her back and pinned her hands on either side of her. "I didn't say it was a bad thing," Sawyer said as his lips traveled along her collarbone.

"But just in case it is, I'll give you something else to think about."

He grazed her skin with his tongue, running it along her neck, then down to the valley of her breasts. Paxton could lose herself in the sensation of that decadent mouth, but it was the solid length of flesh steadily hardening against her stomach that had the power to make her lose her mind. As he continued to tease her with his lips, teeth and tongue, Sawyer deftly lifted her right leg over his shoulder and swiftly entered her body.

Paxton's eyes fell shut as she concentrated on the sensation of having him inside her. The slow, deep slide of his thick erection; the heady, addicting feeling of being stretched with each thrust. His teeth skimmed over her nipple before he sucked it into his mouth and tugged hard.

She clutched his head to her chest, her back arching as she gave herself over to him. She needed him to feel how much she wanted to give him. She wanted him to have all of her. Everything.

Sawyer caught her hips and quickened his pace, plunging in and out with rapid thrusts, sending her completely over the edge within seconds.

He rolled off her and collapsed on the bed, his deep breaths renting the stillness surrounding them. Paxton stared up at the ceiling, her body pulsing with the delicious aftermath of her soul-shattering climax. But even as she basked in the afterglow of Sawyer's lovemaking, she couldn't help the sense of dread that stole over her.

How would she survive the heartache when her fairy tale ended and she returned to her life in Little Rock next week?

Paxton didn't know what to make of Sawyer's mood as they toured the purported site of the levee system that was scheduled to begin construction in a few months. She knew he didn't like Clay, but for once her obnoxious coworker was not being his obnoxious self. Yet Sawyer still seemed…off.

As they toured the site, the representative from the Army Corps of Engineers told them the story of how the entire town of Cairo, which was located just south of here, where the Mississippi and Ohio Rivers met, had been evacuated several years ago. A levee had been purposely breeched in order to save the town from disaster.

As their tour guide pointed out the specifics of the flood protection system, Sawyer's mood continued to darken. She looked at him with a raised brow, but he simply folded his arms over his chest and continued to pout.

Once they were done and on their way back to the rental car, she asked, "You want to share what has you so pissy?"

"You think I'm being pissy?" he asked.

"You refused to even speak to the engineer who was gracious enough to show us around today. Yes, I'd call that being pissy."

"He fed you a load of bull," Sawyer said.

Paxton stopped with her hand on the door. "What are you talking about?"

"All this talk of how great this new levee system will be? It's bull. What he didn't point out is what it will do to the farmland and wildlife just a few miles southwest of here," Sawyer said. He folded his arms over the top of the car and stared at her. "I've seen it before," he said.

Paxton frowned. She thought for a second, and then her eyes widened with understanding. "Did you work here while you lived in Illinois?"

Sawyer nodded. "On this very site."

"Why didn't you say anything?"

He shook his head. "I try not to even think about this project. It's not something I'm proud of."

Paxton walked around to where he stood and leaned against the back driver's side door. "Okay," she said. "Spill."

"I really don't want to talk about this, Pax."

"You should have told me before we even got on the plane to fly up here. Tell me what happened," she prodded.

Sawyer released a sigh and turned around, assuming the same pose she'd taken. He leaned against the door and folded his arms across his chest.

"We decided on the levee design because it was more cost-effective. A controlled breach isn't very hard to fix, if done correctly. It wasn't until we were in the construction phase that I recognized the unintended consequences. Our scope was too narrow. We didn't take into account that our system would push water into several of the smaller surrounding towns."

He looked over at her. The haunted look on his face sent a chill down Paxton's spine. "I think that's exactly what happened to Gauthier."

That chill turned even more frigid. "What do you mean?"

"I think the flood protection system that was constructed around New Orleans following Hurricane Katrina may have contributed to how rapidly the topography in Gauthier has changed. Because of the way the water is being diverted, it's channeling waters at a more rapid pace and cutting grooves into the landscape where it wasn't cut before."

"Even though Landreaux Creek feeds from the Pearl River?"

"I think it's a combination of the wind pushing the waters up from Lake Borgne, along with the river flow. Because of the new levee walls, water pushed back into the tributaries and flooded places that had never flooded before."

Her breath caught in her lungs at the simplicity of his explanation and at how easily it had been missed.

"My goodness, Sawyer. This could change the entire project. Why are you just bringing this up?"

"Because the last time I brought it up it caused another city to lose its flood protection system altogether. When I pointed out the problems with the levee breach design, the Corps halted the project. It was pushed back by more than a year. In that time there was a flood and several people lost their homes. I took a gamble that they couldn't have another huge flood event so soon, and the community paid for it."

"That's why you were so adamant about the maps and making sure the people in Gauthier have the flood insurance they need."

He nodded. "It's also why I want to make sure we've looked at every possibility before this project moves to the next stage."

"Even if it means that Clay comes out ahead of me," Paxton said.

"I don't want—"

She cut him off. "This is about Gauthier. My career is important to me, but there is nothing more important than seeing this project through."

She grabbed the keys to the rental car from his hand

and pushed him aside so that she could get behind the wheel. "Come on," she called. "We've got work to do."

Their flight back to New Orleans was scheduled to leave in less than two hours. She drove the rental car directly to the airport, and, three and a half hours later, they landed at Louis Armstrong International.

Paxton turned her phone back on as soon as the plane's rubber tires hit the tarmac. She had a missed call from Belinda, a text message from Shayla with a picture of her new shelf filled with apple butter and two missed calls from John.

She decided to ignore them all and instead talked strategy with Sawyer for the hour-long drive from the airport to Gauthier. It was after six by the time they arrived. They stopped over in Maplesville for Chinese takeout, which they brought to Sawyer's house.

While he set up the dining room table so that they could work while eating, Paxton finally returned the missed calls and messages, calling Belinda first, then Shayla. She saved her boss for last, hoping that the call would go straight to his voice mail, but he answered on the second ring.

When she finally disconnected the call, she just stood there for a minute staring at it, her mind reeling.

"What's up?" Sawyer asked. He walked over to her. "Pax?"

She looked up at him.

"John wants to pull me off the flood protection project," she said. "I have to leave Gauthier by Sunday morning."

Chapter 11

Sawyer's stomach plummeted.

He moved in closer to her, but she was still staring at the phone as if it held the answer to a riddle.

She finally looked up at him, her eyes bright with enthusiasm. "I can't believe it, Sawyer! This is awesome."

Awesome?

"The funding finally came through on a project I've been working on for nearly three years," Paxton said. "It stalled because of opposition it faced from several advocacy groups, but apparently they worked something out with the state and the project is back on."

Sawyer swallowed deeply before asking, "What's the project?"

"It's a computer-operated hydraulic barrier system in South Carolina. It will be the first of its kind in the country. It's based on a system that was developed by the Dutch, so the first few months will require me to work in the Netherlands."

"So you're going to the Netherlands?"

She nodded. "For two months. The team from Little Rock leaves next week." The smile that broke out across her face was a mile wide. "Do you know what this means for my career, Sawyer? There are as many as a dozen states considering a flood protection system like this one, from New Jersey to the California coast. If I can lead my team to success with the South Carolina project, I will put Bolt-Myer on the map. It can lead to hundreds of millions in contracts and a huge leap for me within the company."

Her excitement was like a punch to the gut. Sawyer knew how much her career meant to her, how hard she'd worked to make a name for herself in the industry. But to see the exhilaration in her eyes as she excitedly talked about leaving made Sawyer want to punch the wall.

Dammit! He wasn't ready to let her go.

"What about *this* project?" Sawyer asked.

Her eyes widened, her dubious expression telling him that she hadn't even considered how her leaving would affect all that they'd strived to accomplish these past weeks.

"Bolt-Myer is sending in another project manager to work with you this week. Perry Conner. He's more than capable of helping you finish up the revised initial concept package."

"What about Gauthier?" Sawyer asked. Her brow furrowed, which made him angry. "You said it yourself, Paxton. No one is going to care about this project as much as we do, because we both love this town and the people who live here. Is this Conner guy going to care whether or not the absolute best job is done, or is Gauthier going to be like any other little town to him? I can't believe after all we've done to save this town from disaster that you would just pick up and leave."

"Sawyer, don't," she bit out.

"Don't? Don't bring up the fact that you're leaving your community in a lurch?"

"That is completely unfair. This is my career we're talking about here."

"Yeah, and apparently your career means more to you than Gauthier does."

Her jaw stiffened with contempt. "You son of a bitch. How dare you try to make me feel guilty for wanting to do what's best for my career?"

"If that's what it takes to make you see the mistake you're making."

"You don't get the right to make me feel guilty. That silver spoon you were born with negates your right to tell me anything when it comes to my hard work."

"Of course." Sawyer threw his hands up. "Here we go with the spoiled-rich-boy rant. I knew you would bring that up."

"You're damn right I will. You don't know what I've had to sacrifice—what I've had to endure in order to get where I am in my career, Sawyer. This project means everything to me."

"The same way your mother's bar means everything to her," he said. "And the way the Lion's Hall means everything to the people who have to bring their kids there for after-school day care. And the way the shelter means everything to all those animals that count on it for survival. It's not just about you and your career, Paxton. This project was supposed to mean more."

She crossed her arms over her chest and stared him down with a dark, cynical expression. "That's really easy for someone who has never had to work for anything."

His head jerked back. "Excuse me?"

"You work because you want to. You never had to," she said. "You can give up this job tomorrow, and it would just be business as usual for you. You don't have to worry about your next meal or keeping a roof over your head or any of the other things that a person like me could never count on."

She stepped up to him, getting right in his face. "You want to know why we could never work, Sawyer? Because it doesn't matter how many times I try to explain it, you will never understand my life and what I've had to live through just to make it to the next day. You will never fully know what it feels like to wonder if you'll get to eat when you wake up in the morning, or if the electric company finally decided to cut the lights off, or if one slow night at Harlon's Bar means that your family won't have enough money to pay the note on a crappy single-wide trailer that cost less than that fancy truck you used to drive.

"So, yes, I'm leaving tomorrow, because my future isn't secured by a trust fund. It requires hard work and sacrifice and tough choices. It's not always pretty, but it's what I've had to deal with my entire life. Welcome to my world, Sawyer."

She picked up her bag and walked out of the house without another word.

"The Netherlands?"

The look of hurt on Shayla's face was enough to make

Paxton's stomach churn, but it was nothing compared with Belinda's dour expression.

"Honestly," Paxton said as she poured whiskey into a highball glass, "it's not a huge deal. It's only for two months."

"But it's halfway around the world," Shayla said.

A crack of thunder rent the air, punctuating her words. The rain had been relentless, pouring from the sky over the past two hours without a break.

"When you think about it, my being in the Netherlands won't be all that different from being in Little Rock. I can still call and email and web chat the same way I do when I'm in Arkansas."

"Yes, but if there's an emergency, you can't just get in your car and drive home," Belinda pointed out.

"What kind of emergency do you expect?" Paxton asked.

As if answering her question, the thunder cracked again, followed by blinding lightning that streaked through the windows. Heinz, who she'd let into the bar once the rain really started to come down, stood and twirled around three times before nestling again at her feet.

"It's two months," Paxton said. "I've explained to both of you how much this project means to me. Why can't you just be happy for me?"

Shayla and her mother both pouted like schoolgirls who'd been denied recess.

"What does Sawyer have to say about this?" Shayla asked.

Just hearing his name made Paxton feel as if her chest was caving in on itself. She didn't want to even think about Sawyer right now. It hurt too damn much.

Donovan, who had been in the kitchen helping Jessie clean out the grease trap since there were so few people in the bar tonight, picked that moment to come up to them, his black gloves covered in grease. If she didn't know for a fact that it would give him the completely wrong impression, Paxton would have kissed him for giving her an excuse to ignore Shayla's question.

"Need something?" Belinda asked him.

"Just looking for—" he reached behind her "—this," he finished, holding up the tire iron Harlon had put behind the bar to deter the occasional drunken fight. It had never been used, but Belinda considered it a part of the scenery, so it remained.

"Why do you need that?" Paxton asked him.

"My baseball cap fell behind the stove. I need something to hook it with." He winked at her. "Thanks for being concerned."

She, Shayla and Belinda all rolled their eyes at him.

When Paxton turned back around, she found her best friend staring at her.

"What?" Paxton asked defensively.

"You really thought I would let it drop? How long have you been knowing me, girl?"

"Just give it a rest." Paxton sighed. She turned and started straightening the liquor bottles that lined the back wall, but she could see Shayla staring back at her in the mirror behind the bar. She spun around to face her. Better to just get this over with.

"Why does it matter what Sawyer says?" Paxton asked.

"Because it does," Belinda said. "You can't just pick up and leave him like this."

Paxton looked at her mother as if she were an alien. "Are you kidding me? You don't even like Sawyer!"

"I never said I didn't like him. I just didn't trust him," Belinda said. "But he's grown on me."

"Really?" Paxton huffed out a laugh.

"He's not a bad person, Paxton. Just look at what he's doing with that building on Highway 22."

Her forehead scrunched in confusion. "The one with the green shutters that's been vacant for years? What is he doing with it?"

"He didn't tell you?" Shayla asked. Paxton shook her head. "He's turning it into a rec center. At first it was only supposed to be for employees at the lumber mill, but, according to Mike Bastian, Sawyer's making it into a rec center that will be open for everyone in Landreaux so that the kids in this area don't have to travel all the way into town."

Paxton remembered what she'd told him during their tour of the Lion's Club, and her heart melted on the spot. Damn him for always doing the absolute sweetest thing.

Thunder cracked with enough force to shake the building. Moments later, the front door of the bar flew open. Harlon came in dressed in a yellow rain slicker.

"We need all hands on deck," he called. "Tell Donovan to get his butt out here."

Paxton raced from around the bar. "What's going on?" she asked Harlon.

He shook his head. "Too much rain in too short of a time. The creek is flooding. Some of the homes on Sandalwood are already taking in water."

"On Sandalwood?" Shayla asked.

"The animal shelter," Paxton whispered. "We need to go."

Paxton ran to the kitchen and grabbed her raincoat from the hook, calling out to Donovan to come along. She convinced Belinda to stay behind to watch the bar; then she and Shayla hopped into her car, following behind Harlon's beat-up Chevy.

They had to park at the head of Sandalwood Drive, which was at a slightly lower elevation and known to flood even before this weird flooding phenomenon had started to take place. The flashing lights of several emergency vehicles could be seen, along with a short flatbed truck stacked high with sandbags.

"We started filling these after Tropical Storm Lucy," Harlon called over the crack of yet more thunder.

They all joined in with the people shuttling sandbags in an assembly line. It seemed as if it would take a million of them to stave off the water streaming in from the toppling creek, but with every sandbag that fell into her waiting arms, Paxton knew it was potentially another pet saved, another home spared.

The rain sluiced down the slick blacktopped roadway, running in swift rivulets. She'd never seen anything like this in Gauthier. The sight caused chills to cascade down her spine as powerfully as the water down the street.

"We've gotta move faster," Donovan called as he tossed another sandbag her way.

They continued their coordinated assembly line, the water reaching their ankles. Headlights shone as several other cars pulled up to the head of the street.

Paxton peered through the darkness and spotted Sawyer running toward them. Her heart flip-flopped within her chest. He acknowledged her with a slight nod before jogging past the assembly line toward the animal shelter. He returned minutes later with a pet carrier tucked under each arm. Webster Detellier followed behind, also burdened down by animals.

They worked for two hours straight, hauling sandbags and pets, until they finally had some control over the water. By the time they were done the rain had slowed to a steady but much less powerful downfall.

Members of the community huddled in the street, talking strategy for how to clean up the mess in the houses that had taken in water. Thankfully, only four on this street, along with the animal shelter, had seen any accumulation. And, thankfully, that had only been about two inches, not even enough to reach the top edge of the baseboards, so at least they wouldn't have to rip out any walls.

As she held a shivering cocker spaniel and poodle mix in her arms, Paxton couldn't help the tears that began to stream down her face. The adrenaline from the past few hours had worn off, leaving her drained, her emotions raw and exposed.

Not a single photo or secondhand story could tell the full picture of exactly what this town was up against. Tonight, she'd seen it with her own eyes; she'd felt the anxiety and desperation deep in her bones.

And, just like that, Paxton made her decision.

"I need you."

Sawyer turned at the sound of Paxton's breathless plea. Droplets of the still-misting rain peppered her smooth brown skin, making it glisten under the gleam of the streetlights overhead.

"What?" he asked, wondering if he'd heard her wrong.

"I said I need you." She held her hands out in helpless appeal. "I need to see this project through to the end,

Sawyer. I can't leave Gauthier without making sure it's done right. Not after what I saw tonight. But I need your help. If we work all night, we can get the revised ICP done before I leave."

"So, you're still leaving," he said, the truth crushing his soul all over again.

"Yes, I am. I *have* to." She paused, then said, "But you can come with me."

His body went rigid, his eyes narrowing in confusion.

"Just hear me out," she said. "The Army Corps's Charleston district is sending three engineers to the Netherlands with us to study this system. I know you can make a case with the New Orleans office to come with us. We can make this work, Sawyer."

He cursed the thread of hope blossoming in his chest, but he couldn't fight it. Still, he managed to keep his expression neutral as he glanced toward the activity taking place at the animal shelter before looking back at her. Clearing his throat, Sawyer said, "When you say that we can make *this* work, what exactly are you talking about, Paxton? The project, or—"

"Everything," she said. She stared at him, her eyes soft and full of naked honestly. She closed the distance between them and took his hands in hers. "I'm stubborn and hardheaded and when I get mad at you I'll probably say some things that I regret, but if you're willing to put up with me, I will gladly hand over my heart to you, Sawyer. In fact, you already have it."

Sawyer wrapped his arms around her and pulled her to him.

"It's an even swap," he said. "You've had my heart for longer than you can possibly know." He pressed a kiss to her forehead, then lifted her chin so he could look her in the eyes. "I've got a fresh bag of coffee grounds from the Jazzy Bean. What do you say we tear it open and get to work?"

She smiled up at him. "That sounds like a plan."

Once they established that everything was under control on Sandalwood Drive, Paxton checked in with Shayla, letting her know that she was leaving with Sawyer.

The rain continued to fall in a light mist as they drove over the bridge and into downtown Gauthier. Sawyer pulled into his garage and popped open his trunk, where he kept duplicates of the maps that were currently on the walls of the conference room in the Gauthier Law Firm. Everything else they needed was on his computer.

He placed several maps in Paxton's waiting arms and ushered her toward the door. Then they spread everything out over the dining room table.

Sawyer looked over at her, still drenched from the rain, her short hair plastered to her forehead.

"You have no idea how badly I want to strip you naked and haul you to my bed, but I know it has to wait."

Her gaze traveled appreciatively down his body. "It can be our reward for all of our hard work."

"God, yes," he said. "We're getting this done tonight, and then spending the next two days locked in this house with no clothes on. I'm not letting you wear clothes in the Netherlands, either."

"You've got yourself a deal," Paxton said.

Sawyer made coffee, and, armed with caffeine, they began the arduous task of writing up the revised initial concept package report. Sawyer had always considered this part of the project to be an exercise in bureaucratic red tape, but after the inaccurate topography map discovery, and the mess they'd witnessed tonight with the flooding on Sandalwood Drive, he would never think of the review stage in the same way again. He had never been more confident that the work he and Paxton had put in over the past few weeks would save more property in this town—and possibly even some lives.

"The recommendation portion will probably be the most difficult to write," Paxton said.

"Don't second-guess yourself," Sawyer told her. "You've studied this project. You know it inside and out, Pax."

"Can we do it together?" she asked.

Sawyer nodded. After putting aside his coffee, he walked over to where she was sitting on his chaise lounge, the same chaise where they'd made love several nights ago. He planned to make love to her in that very spot again once they were done with this.

Putting thoughts of the hot sex in his near future out of his head, Sawyer studied the computer screen on her lap. Together, they drafted their opinion of what would be the best fit for the Gauthier flood protection system. Even though it was not part of the official proposal requirements, Paxton insisted that they include a section on some of the potential unexpected consequences that could arise if they built the flood protection wall to the specs laid out in the ICP by the Bolt-Myer engineers. In the end, they recommended a new system with slight modifications, including floodgate walls along the lowest banks of Landreaux Creek.

Paxton saved the document to the hard drive and a separate flash drive, and then emailed copies to both herself and Sawyer's personal email.

"I say we go over this one more time tomorrow, just to make sure we didn't forget anything."

"That sounds good to me," Sawyer said. He moved a wisp of short hair from her neck. "But you know what sounds even better?"

"A shower?"

He tilted his head to the side. "Yeah, a shower would work with what I have in mind."

Paxton turned on the chaise, placing each of her thighs over his. She grabbed the hem of his shirt and raised it over his head. "Okay, let's get just a bit dirtier before we take that shower."

"I can definitely work with that," Sawyer said. He stopped, placing his hand over hers. "I just have one promise I need you to make."

"What's that?"

"That you'll stay with me forever. No more running away, Pax. I don't care where we are in the world, physically, but I want you here." He pointed to his chest. "I need you here with me. Always."

She leaned forward and, with her lips against his, whispered, "There is nowhere else I'd rather be."

* * * * *

This summer is going to be hot, hot, hot
with a new miniseries
from fan-favorite authors!

YAHRAH ST. JOHN
LISA MARIE PERRY
PAMELA YAYE

HEAT WAVE
OF DESIRE

HOT SUMMER
NIGHTS

HEAT OF
PASSION

Available June 2015 *Available July 2015* *Available August 2015*

California Desert Dreams

Their affair is this exclusive resort's best-kept secret

HEAT of PASSION

PAMELA YAYE

Robyn Henderson, Belleza Resort's head event planner, is throwing the charity event of the season. But when a series of bizarre incidents hit, evidence points to LA restaurateur Sean Parker, Robyn's secret crush—and her best friend's brother. As Sean fights to clear his name, he must decide where his future lies. But can he also convince Robyn to trust in their love?

California Desert Dreams

"A compelling page-turner from start to finish."
—*RT Book Reviews* on *SEDUCED BY MR. RIGHT*

HARLEQUIN®
www.Harlequin.com

Available August 2015!

KPPY4130815

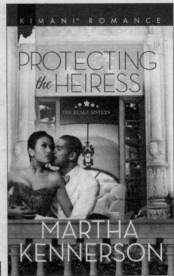

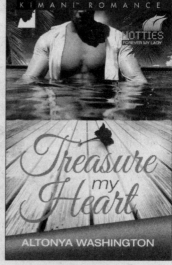

REQUEST YOUR FREE BOOKS!

2 FREE NOVELS
PLUS 2 FREE GIFTS!

KIMANI™
ROMANCE

Love's ultimate destination!

BESTSELLING AUTHOR COLLECTION

CLASSIC ROMANCES IN COLLECTIBLE VOLUMES

New York Times **Bestselling Author**

BRENDA JACKSON

Sometimes a knight in shining armor wears a cowboy hat

Seven years ago, as a young cop, Darius Franklin saved a vulnerable woman from a violent situation. They shared one night of pure passion before she walked away. Now Darius is a wealthy rancher and security contractor working at a women's shelter. And he's shocked to meet the new social worker: Summer Martindale, a beautiful damsel no longer in distress.

ONE NIGHT WITH THE WEALTHY RANCHER

"Brenda Jackson writes romance that sizzles and characters you fall in love with." —*New York Times* bestselling author Lori Foster

Available August 2015 wherever books are sold!

www.Harlequin.com

NYTBJ0815